THE
LAST MAN'S
REWARD

David Patneaude

ALBERT WHITMAN & COMPANY
MORTON GROVE, ILLINOIS

Library of Congress Cataloging-in-Publication Data

Patneaude, David.
    The last man's reward / David Patneaude.
        p. cm.
    Summary: In hopes of winning the valuable baseball card that he and
his new friends have hidden in a remote cave outside Granite Falls,
Washington, Albert asks the gruff P.E. teacher at his middle school to
help him become a long-jumper.
    ISBN 0-8075-4370-5
    [1. Friendship—Fiction. 2. Teacher-student relationships—Fiction.
3. Baseball cards—Fiction.] I. Title.

PZ7.P2734Las   1996   95-32095
[Fic]—dc20   CIP
                                                               AC

Published in 1996 by Albert Whitman & Company,
6340 Oakton Street, Morton Grove, Illinois 60053-2723.
Published simultaneously in Canada by General Publishing, Limited,
Toronto.
Printed in the United States of America.
10

Design by Lindaanne Donohoe.
The text of this book is set in Stone Serif.

To Judy,
who brings out the best in me,
and
to Judith,
who brings out the best in my writing.

Also by David Patneaude

Someone Was Watching

Dark Starry Morning:
Stories of this world and beyond

Framed In Fire

Haunting at Home Plate

Hey, Alibi! You tired yet?" Albert looked up and saw Nick glance back, grinning, from the lead position. Despite snickers from the other bike riders, Albert ignored him. He was used to Nick by now.

"Huh, Alibi?" Nick said. "Those skinny legs of yours need a rest?"

"Wiry," Albert said. "I call them wiry. As in steel." More snickers. "How's your mouth, Sponge Brain?" he said. "Tired yet?" He heard Yuno force a laugh. Not much of a laugh, but better than nothing.

Nick accelerated. As usual, everyone else followed their leader, strung together like boxcars behind a runaway engine. Albert leaned forward, pedaling hard, staying close but not moving out of the order. He knew his place by now, earned over the hundreds of miles they'd put in during the summer. He was content that he wasn't last. And he wasn't about to let Yuno, who was struggling noisily to keep up, move past him in the pecking order—ever.

Albert turned his baseball cap around to keep it from flying off and tried to concentrate on the ride.

Nick, the self-proclaimed leader, had dreamed up nicknames for everyone else; he hadn't given himself one. Albert had dubbed him Sponge Brain, but it hadn't caught on.

Behind Nick was Mike "Princess" Dye, who had come all the way from England. Mike wasn't very fond of royalty—or his nickname.

Next in line rode Joey Zemo, who'd grown up in Wyoming. On the day Joey'd moved into the apartment complex, Albert and Nick saw him being chased onto the hood of a parked car by a shoebox-sized dog with legs the length of pickles. Nick soon had a name for Joey: Small Dog.

Albert thought "Alibi" wasn't the worst of the lot, although he wasn't happy with the reason he got the name. So what if he liked to read? So what if his excuses for staying in his apartment hadn't been real good? It wasn't that he didn't like to horse around or get into sports. It was just that reading was an inside, solitary kind of thing.

Behind Albert was Lester "Yuno" Lambert, who had pretty much earned his own alias. Nearly every sentence from his mouth contained at least one "you know."

By now this trip was a ritual. The first time, two months ago, it had been just a spur-of-the-moment idea. On one of the first nice days of summer, Nick had asked Albert, Princess, and Yuno if they wanted to ride their bikes to a pool on the Stillaguamish River for a day of swimming. Albert wasn't too sure at first. Fourteen miles, mostly uphill, sounded like a long trip, especially on legs more accustomed to traveling in a car. But he wanted to make friends—his old friends were two hundred miles away in Portland—so he said yes.

They saw the countryside and swam and explored. They built a raft that sank like a submarine. Mostly, they laughed a lot. They had such a good time that they went back the next day. And the day after. And the day after that. They'd hardly missed a day since.

A week after they started going, Joey moved in, and Albert asked him if he wanted to come along. He did, and that was it; that was the group. Five boys whose families had just moved to this small Washington town had come together to make the most of their situation.

And they were doing it, even though none of them would have chosen to be here if they'd had a choice. They'd given up friends and familiar schools and homes of their own. They'd come to a place of strangers and strange schools and temporary, company-sponsored housing in the Riverbend Apartments, where everything was clean and modern but nothing seemed like home. They were here because their dads or moms had taken jobs with SoftEdge.

The giant software company had pulled up its shallow roots from the congestion of Seattle's eastern suburbs and moved north to Granite Falls for fresh air and growing room. SoftEdge built its sprawling facility just outside the old city limits.

The boys left trees and pastures behind them and reached the original section of Granite Falls. They sped past the quiet storefronts of the old business district, past old houses in old neighborhoods, and rounded off a sharp "L" in the road. They whipped past Granite Falls Middle School, Albert's everyday destination in less than a month. He tried not to look at it. He wasn't ready to think about school yet.

If they had been biking here before SoftEdge arrived, they already would have been out of town. Now they just changed neighborhoods, old to new. Wide streets branched off the main highway. The entrance to each street had the name of a housing development on a big, rustic sign. WHISPERWOOD, the first one said; MOUNTAIN VISTA, the next one. Houses and condominiums and apartments could be glimpsed through the trees.

They pushed on, and Albert felt himself running out of gas. He shouldn't have tried to finish that book the night before. But he wasn't about to tell Nick to slow down. It was the kind of complaint that Nick would turn into a nasty barb in no time. No, Albert would keep his mouth shut. He could maintain this pace as long as any of the other guys could.

He glanced behind him, making sure Yuno hadn't gained any ground. Head down, Yuno was pedaling furiously, his shorter legs and pudgy body working as hard as they could. "I think I can," Albert heard him say between gasps.

Albert could see the entrance to the last housing development a block away. A woman was hammering something onto the streetsign post.

MOVING SALE, the sign said. Nothing important. But he was tired, and that made up his mind for him.

"Moving sale, Nick!" he yelled out, trying to sound excited rather than exhausted.

"So?" Nick shot back, easing off on the pedals.

Albert had to come up with something good—something other than he needed a break. He thought for a moment, his mind racing.

"Baseball cards!" he blurted out. If anything could make Nick stop, that was it.

Nick stopped ten feet from the woman. The others coasted up.

"Baseball cards, huh, Alibi?" Nick said, barely breathing hard. "Or did you just need a rest?" He looked at Albert, waiting for an answer, while the other boys glanced back and forth, not sure whose side to take.

Albert decided that he wasn't the only one who was tired.

"Or did you just want to look for some books?" Nick made the word sound like some slimy, smelly, unrecognizable object that the dog had dragged in. Certainly not something any normal person would like.

"There really could, you know, be some baseball cards, Nick," Yuno said.

Having Yuno stick up for you was about as cool as letting Nick catch you reading a book, or belonging to the Chess Club.

But books, now. The idea of a treasury of used books was something that definitely did appeal to him.

"I have some," she said softly, looking at Albert curiously. He stared back at her, wondering how she'd known what he was thinking. She brushed a wisp of brown hair from her forehead and pushed her shirt sleeves up.

"Books?" Nick said. "You've got books for sale?"

"And baseball cards," she said.

Nick grinned, but avoided looking at Albert. "Yes!" he said.

"You really do have baseball cards?" Small Dog asked.

"A whole tackle box full," she said.

"A big tackle box?" Nick asked.

"A very big tackle box."

"For sale?" Small Dog said.

She nodded. "For sale."

Albert glanced at Princess, who was watching the conversation with amusement. He still didn't understand the fascination with cardboard pictures of men who played a silly game and spit tobacco.

"Is your kid selling 'em?" Nick said. His voice was suddenly a notch higher, his breathing quick and shallow.

She looked at Albert. "Is your friend always this excitable?"

"Sometimes he's worse."

She smiled. "My kid isn't selling the cards. I am."

"Can we see them?" Albert said.

"Sure," she said. "You guys can be my first customers. I'm just a few blocks away, if you want to follow me on your bikes."

n two minutes she pulled up in front of a nice two-story house that looked much like the other nice two-story houses they'd passed. A SOLD sign sprouted from the front lawn. In the garage was an assortment of furniture, boxes of lawn tools, sporting goods, and other items that people accumulate.

"My name's Maggie," she said, hurrying up behind them. "If you guys will help me get this stuff into the driveway, I'll dig out those baseball cards. The exercise will be good for you, anyway," she said, grinning.

Now Albert understood: the old Tom Sawyer routine. Did she really think they were stupid enough to fall for something that obvious?

Before she could finish her last sentence, Nick was in the garage, and in an instant he was joined by the other three. Even Princess, who didn't know Mickey Mantle from Mickey Mouse, was helping. Albert stayed where he was.

Maggie gave him a questioning look.

"I read *Tom Sawyer*," he said. "Twice."

She looked at him blankly. "Oh—you think I—" She laughed, a nice, easy laugh. "I just thought as long as you were here—but I suppose it seems like I planned it, doesn't it?"

"Uh-huh." Albert still wasn't sure she hadn't. Until she smiled again. Then he was convinced. He walked into the garage. By the time he and Princess horsed out all the bedroom furniture, the other guys had emptied the rest of the garage and were standing next to some likely looking boxes in the driveway.

"Thanks, fellas." Maggie pulled back the flaps on one box, grabbed out several books—*books*, Albert thought—and shook her head. "Wrong box." She looked at Albert, but he pretended not to notice. He could come back later. By himself.

But Nick had noticed. "Something for you, Alibi."

"And maybe she has some coloring books for you, Sponge Brain," Albert said.

"Yeah," said Yuno. "And maybe, you know, some crayons."

"No coloring books, no crayons," Maggie said. "No kids," she added, almost to herself.

She peeked inside a second box, and then a third, and Albert was beginning to wonder if she even had cards. Maybe his Tom Sawyer theory was right after all.

"Aha!" She opened up the fourth and hoisted out a huge metal tackle box. She swung it awkwardly onto a table, which wobbled with the extra weight.

Albert watched the guys converge on the box, attracted like steel shavings to a giant magnet. He pushed his way into the group. Nick flipped up the latch. Albert wondered who was going to make first claim on the cards. He thought he knew.

Slowly, reverently, Nick lifted the lid, revealing a package wrapped in thick brown paper.

Small Dog and Nick eased the package onto the table.

Nick gently tore away a section of tape, spreading the paper apart beneath it, just far enough for a look.

He lifted out a card. Before anyone else could see it, he popped it back in the package and smoothed down the paper and tape.

Albert had watched Nick's eyes grow wide. Now Nick was taking too much time with the package so he wouldn't have to look up and give himself away.

"How much do you want for these, uh, Maggie?" Nick asked. The words came out in a croak. His hands kept stroking and patting the package. He began shifting his weight from foot to foot. Albert thought Nick was about to wet his pants.

"The whole box, you mean?" she said, looking amused.

Nick nodded and pulled the package closer, shielding it from reach.

"Aren't you going to look at the rest?" she asked.

"I'll take my chances," Nick said.

"What's this 'I' stuff?" Albert said. "We've got just

as much right to the cards as you do."

Yuno chirped up. "Yeah, Nick. What's this 'I' stuff?"

"Yeah, Nick," Small Dog and Princess said in unison.

"I thought you guys were friends," said Maggie.

They fidgeted, letting her comment dangle in the air.

"We are," Nick said finally.

"Then I think you should be able to share in the purchase." She paused for a moment. "If you want to buy them. How much do you think they're worth, Nick? You had a peek."

Nick's face moved through a whole series of contortions. "The one I saw was worth about seven dollars."

Albert was sure he was telling the truth. He could see it in Nick's eyes.

"And how many cards do you think there are?" Maggie asked.

Albert started running estimates through his mind.

"Quite a few," Nick said.

"Hundreds," Albert said, seeing their chances of buying the cards reducing from unlikely to zilch.

"So do you think there might be one more seven-dollar card in the collection?"

They all looked at her as if she'd just asked whether they'd find cheese in a pizza parlor.

"Chances are," Nick said.

"Probably several more." Albert knew there was no point in being cute about it. But Nick gave him a dirty look.

"Probably a lot more." Yuno smiled at Albert. Nick shifted his glare to Yuno, who ignored him.

"A whole pile of 'em," Small Dog said.

"A bloody tackling box full." Princess looked pleased with himself.

"Tackle box," Albert said. "For fishing."

Maggie laughed. "You guys wouldn't do very well buying a used car, but I think you all agree that there's probably at least one more seven-dollar card."

They nodded their heads.

"So why don't I make it fourteen dollars?"

Albert watched looks of surprise cross the guys' faces as her words registered.

"Two times seven's still fourteen, isn't it?" she asked.

"It is." Nick reached in his pocket. "It is," he said again, as the others fumbled in theirs. "Two times seven. It makes sense."

"Not when there could be two *hundred* seven-dollar cards," Albert said. "Or even some better ones." He felt an elbow in his ribs and ignored it. "Why only fourteen dollars?"

"A long story." Her smile faded. "Let's just say my

ex-husband found other interests. He asked me to sell his things for him."

"But won't he be mad?" Albert said.

"I hope so," she said, looking as if she meant it. "What do you guys think? Am I being too harsh?"

Everyone stared at her, then at the ground, too embarrassed to answer.

"I hope you guys see a lesson in this story."

"Don't ever let your wife get your baseball cards," Nick said, grinning.

"Well," she said, ignoring Nick, "if you guys are done examining my motives, I think it's time to show me your money."

They all had some money, but they only came up with a total of $12.75.

Nick looked at Maggie. "One of us can ride home real quick and—"

"Close enough," she said.

She held out her hand, and they filled it with money. She shook each one of their hands.

Albert was the only one with a rack on the back of his bike, so he was given the honor of transporting the cards. After they'd carefully slid the package back into the tackle box and fastened the lid, they set it on the rack. Maggie gave them some twine to secure it.

"You sure you won't fall, Alibi?" Nick said, as he checked the box for the third time.

Albert couldn't believe him. "You want to ride my bike?" He watched Nick pause.

"No, you go ahead. But be careful."

Albert had just turned toward the street when a car pulled up and blocked most of the driveway. Albert aimed his bike at the narrow space left and swung his leg over the bar, ready to head out.

"Mr. Rockwood," he heard Nick say from somewhere behind him. Something in the way he said it made Albert stop in his tracks.

The driver got out, unfolding his long, wiry body until he stood tall next to the small blue sedan. Albert could hear his own heart thumping.

The man smiled. His eyes were an icy blue. His hair was steel gray, cut in a flat-topped buzz. He held his arms slightly away from his body, as if his muscles were too tightly strung to relax, as if he were ready to pounce. Albert put one foot on a pedal, set to ride.

"Mr. Spellman," the man said, starting up the driveway. His voice was low and gravelly, but boomed out ahead of him. "Are you having a good summer?"

"A good summer?" Nick found his voice. "Yeah, I've been having a real good sum—"

"That's nice, Mr. Spellman," Mr. Rockwood said. "You should enjoy it while you can. School will be starting again before you know it."

He kept walking, looking at Maggie now, not

acknowledging the rest of them as he marched past. "These boys behaving themselves this morning, ma'am?" he asked. "Not giving you any trouble, are they?" He stopped at the table and smiled again, his teeth white against skin reddened and weathered by the sun.

"Trouble?" she said. "You mean like robbery or something?" She smiled and shook her head. "You must not know these guys."

"Maybe not," he said. "But I've known a lot of guys just like them."

"Really? *Just* like them? I doubt that."

He stared at her, and she stared right back, until he looked away, at the boxes and piles. "You have any books?" he said.

Albert couldn't believe it. The last thing that he expected was this guy to be looking for books. And now he was going to be picking through Albert's books.

"Children's books, I mean?" he said. "Fairy tales, preferably. Something old, if you have it. Something with a happy ending."

"You might be in luck," Maggie said, heading for the boxes. "I think we have a couple of old books."

"We've gotta go." Nick pushed off without looking back. "Go, Alibi."

Albert started rolling.

"You guys be sure to come back if you decide you

want anything else, okay?" said Maggie. "And bring your parents, if you want."

"Bye, Maggie." Albert waved as he coasted out of the driveway.

"Both hands on the grips," Nick said from behind him. "You can say hi to her when you come back."

"Who's Mr. Rockwood?" Albert asked.

"You'll know soon enough. I don't want to ruin the rest of your summer."

"Really, who is he? The guy's scary."

"P.E. teacher," Nick said finally. "*Your* P.E. teacher."

Albert would have guessed boot camp instructor. Now he really wasn't ready to think about school.

He picked up the pace, waiting for Nick to pass him. But no one passed him. One block slipped by. And another. And then he figured out what was going on: Nick wanted to keep an eye on him.

Albert looked back again. Nick's front wheel was practically touching Albert's rear one. "Back off, Sponge Brain. If you bump me with the box on here, there's no telling what might happen."

It worked. Nick eased back a few feet, and Albert was left alone to enjoy being the leader, for once. Maybe he hadn't earned this spot—yet—but he could pretend as well as anybody. And he was carrying some cargo that wasn't just pretend. He sat tall and let the breeze rush past his face.

THREE

Albert stopped at the entrance to Falls Meadows. "Home?" he asked as the other guys pulled up next to him.

As usual, they were waiting for some kind of decision from Nick. "I don't think so," he said.

"Why not?" Albert asked.

"It's Saturday. Our parents are home."

"So?" Yuno said.

"So, they'll wonder why we're back home already. And where we got the tackle box. And what's in it. And how much the cards are worth. And how much we paid for 'em." Nick paused and looked around. "And then you know what'll happen?"

"They'll make us return them," Princess said.

Albert knew Nick had seen the problems before anyone else had. But he wasn't about to admit it. "The river, then?" he asked with as little enthusiasm as he could manage.

"Yes," Princess said.

"Just like usual," Nick said.

"Okay." Albert turned right and headed up the highway.

He wasn't used to being in the lead; it was different

than following behind Small Dog. And the weight of the tackle box made his bike feel top-heavy. He found himself concentrating more than usual, especially when a car passed and he had to move toward the shoulder.

He'd just begun adjusting to the cars when he heard the roar of a powerful engine behind him. An empty logging truck blew past, its horn blasting. From six feet away he watched the blur of black tires and chrome wheels. The air deadened for an instant and then exploded, swirling around Albert like a small tornado, sucking up dust and leaves and twigs and tossing them twenty feet in the air.

The truck thundered on up the highway. Albert wobbled to a stop and stared at the mudflaps suspended from the rear of the truck's frame. On each flap a snake lay coiled for the strike. And under each serpent were the words, "Don't Tread on Me."

Albert heard Nick laugh behind him—a nervous, forced laugh—but he didn't turn around. He was afraid his face would somehow give away the feeling of panic that had put a huge lump in his throat. He looked up at the mountains ahead, trying to catch his breath.

Nick pulled up next to Albert. "You okay, Alibi?" He strummed the twine holding the tackle box in place.

"I'm fine," he said. He glanced at his precious cargo. "But maybe someone else could lead."

"I'll go first," Small Dog said.

Albert got the feeling that Small Dog was concerned about him, and not the cards. Not *just* the cards, anyway.

"Okay," Albert said. He motioned Small Dog around him.

"Why don't I ride behind everyone else for a while," Nick said. "I can keep an eye out for road hogs and let you know before they get too close."

Albert tried to decide if Nick was being considerate or if he just wanted to protect the cards. Probably the cards. He'd never volunteered to ride caboose before today.

Once they got going again it seemed easier, even when they hit the long incline that slowed them to a crawl. Albert found himself relaxing, synchronizing his efforts with the pumping and breathing of the other riders.

Mile after mile crept by, and at last they topped a final hill and arrived at the big fir that marked the cutoff.

Albert followed Small Dog between the fir and a boulder the size of a small car, down the hundred yards of trail, steep and twisting. He arrived at the sandy beach upright and in one piece. He looked at the pool—the cool, inviting pool. But first he wanted to take care of one other thing.

"Let's open the box," he said.

"Here?" Nick said. "Now?" He forced a laugh, looking at the other guys for support.

Albert could see a confrontation coming. "Why not? Why not here? We all want to see what we bought."

Nick had his argument ready. "What if there's some more good cards in the box, and we get 'em messed up? Besides, I don't have my catalogs with me. All we have to do is wait a few hours."

"And then what will your excuse be?" Albert said. "Suspicious parents? Spies?"

"Nothing. As soon as we get home, we'll open 'em up. What do you say, guys?"

"I think you're a bit of a fanatic," Princess said to Nick, "but I don't mind waiting."

"I can wait," Small Dog said.

Nick had his majority. "Okay," Albert said. "I guess we'll wait. But you can stand guard." He whipped off his hat, shoes, and T-shirt. "I'm going swimming."

Albert sprinted to a huge rock outcropping that formed a deep pool on its upriver side. Downriver, an old cedar tree was nudged tightly against the rock, its lower branches reaching well out over the river, providing shade and one perfectly placed anchor for a length of rope.

Albert scrambled up onto the outcropping and ran

across its flat top. At the edge, he launched himself into the air and grabbed the rope, which hung from a stout branch twenty feet overhead. He felt the air suddenly cool as it rushed past his face. He swung out over the pool, looking down at the glassy water below him, savoring the feeling of floating, of flying, of freedom. He let himself swing back over the rock and saw that the rest of them—everyone but Nick—were up on the rock, shaking themselves out of their clothes. Down at the beach Nick watched him, a grin on his face and one hand resting on the tackle box. Maybe Albert would go back later and relieve him—give Nick a chance to have some fun. Maybe. And maybe he wouldn't.

Albert arched his body at the end of the rope's arc, trying to pump more distance into his flight back over the water. He straightened, waiting for the right moment, feeling the tingle in his stomach. Then he was over the pool again, and he let go. His momentum carried him up, lifted his legs until he hung head-first, feeling for an instant the weightlessness of a space walker. While the water came up below him in slow motion, he saw the other guys jockeying for position on the rock.

Too late, he saw the log.

It had slipped into the pool quickly and silently, like a crocodile on the hunt. It stalled right below Albert, pivoting in a lazy whirlpool, waiting.

He was going to hit it. No time to do anything. Instinct told him to duck, and he did, chin to chest, trying to pull in like a turtle. But he had no shell.

He hit headfirst. The sound—a bat-on-ball—exploded in his ears. The impact rocked his head forward. Pain shot down into his neck and shoulders and tore at his back, sharp at first and then dull, and then gone. Everything was gone. Everything was black.

He awoke to cold—the total cold that comes in mountain water. He was under. Water filled his mouth, his nose, his throat. His chest ached as if he'd been kicked. He told himself to relax, to let his body seek the surface. But his head throbbed, and he couldn't think, and it was taking too long. He had to get air.

He felt something—an arm—around his neck. Somebody was trying to drown him. He struggled—panicky now—but felt himself being towed through the water. Was he being taken down?

No. Up! He stared through the clear, bubbly water and saw sunlight and blue sky. An instant later he burst through the surface, coughing, sneezing, gasping for breath, still struggling against the arm.

"Take it easy, Alibi," a voice said. He twisted his head—his throbbing, aching head—and glimpsed Nick's face behind him. He relaxed, still trying to get his breath, and let Nick tug him toward shore. When he looked toward the rock, he saw Small Dog and

Princess in the water, racing toward him. Yuno stood on the edge, his eyes on Albert, his mouth frozen open. He looked like a frightened statue.

Nick shifted his grip and lifted, and Albert felt sand and rocks—solid bottom—beneath his feet. He stood waist-deep, weak-legged and light-headed, and coughed out a stream of water. For an instant he thought he would throw up. But he swallowed hard and coughed again—a moist, wheezy cough. Droplets of water flew into the air and caught the sunlight before raining down on the surface of the pool.

"You okay?" Nick had a vise hold on Albert's arm. "Do we need to get you to a doctor?"

Albert felt the back of his head. A lump had formed, but it was small. He ran his hand down farther. His neck was tender, probably scratched, but he checked his fingers for blood and found none. He shrugged his shoulders, and they worked. Everything seemed to work.

"I'm okay," he said. Wheeze. "Thanks, Nick." Wheeze. Albert waded toward shore, Small Dog and Princess at his side now, Nick propping him up. He staggered onto the beach and sat. When he opened his eyes, Yuno was there. His face, freckles and all, looked as pale as the puffy clouds drifting overhead.

"Sorry, Alibi," he said.

"For what?" Wheeze.

"I, you know, didn't help."

"No problem." Wheeze. "I had plenty of help."

"Yeah," Yuno said, but he didn't look comforted.

Albert felt a hand on the back of his head, slowly pushing through his hair.

"A bit of a scrape," Princess said. He brought his face close enough to examine Albert's scalp. "A bit of a lump."

"Scraped your back, too," Small Dog said.

"Lucky you didn't hit it square," Nick said.

"Yeah." Albert peered out toward the middle of the pool. The log was gone, moved downstream. He thought about what could have happened—his brains splattered all over it, his neck broken—and he shuddered.

"You need to look next time," Yuno said.

Wheeze. "I'm not jumping anymore today. I'll watch the cards." Albert saw Nick glance toward the tackle box. It looked as if he'd almost forgotten about the cards for a few minutes.

Albert made it to the bike. He sat and rested, and breathed in the life-giving air, and waited for the sun's warmth to make his aches go away. He'd just sit where it was safe, and wait.

Albert sat on the edge of the bed, gingerly fingering the back of his head and neck, as Small Dog closed the bedroom door. Small Dog's parents weren't home, but Small Dog wasn't taking any chances. He pushed his chair up against the door. Nick nodded his approval and set the tackle box on the rug.

Once again, the lid creaked up, and the package slid out.

"Easy," Nick said. "Take it easy."

They lifted the wrapping, and there the cards were. For a moment everyone—even Nick—pulled back, just looking. But Albert knew one thing already: of the fifteen or twenty cards he could see, there were none he'd seen before, except in magazines.

Albert glanced at Nick. "Which one did you look at last time?"

"This one—the Eddie Matthews," Nick said, carefully picking up a card. "Seven dollars—at least—for one in this condition. But I don't see any that aren't worth something."

Nick picked up another one and glanced at the back. "Billy Williams," he said. "Eight dollars, minimum."

Two cards so far, and they already had their money's worth.

Small Dog held up a card. "Tim McCarver. Nineteen sixty-five."

Nick thumbed through his catalog. "Two dollars and seventy-five cents." He shook his head. "Every one of 'em is older than we are."

"And Maggie knew it," said Albert.

"She had to." Princess sounded as if he was starting to get into this baseball card stuff.

"So we're not taking 'em back," Nick said.

Albert shook his head. Nick needed to mellow out a bit. "Nobody said we were, but I think we need to find out exactly what we have. You got some paper and a pen, Small Dog?"

"On the desk."

"Now we need to get the information down," said Albert. "Small Dog and Princess and Yuno—you guys divide up the cards—"

"Carefully," Nick said. "They've got no covers."

"—and then take turns reading 'em off," Albert continued. "Nick can tell us what they're worth, and I'll write 'em down. Okay?" There weren't any objections, although Nick looked as if he was thinking about it. But he had the price lists, and no one else knew the information like he did—his dad had practically raised him on baseball cards.

Under the loose cards on top, three long rows of cards formed the next layer. Princess kept one row and gave one row each, along with the loose cards, to Yuno and Small Dog.

"There's another package under these," Princess said.

Nobody moved.

"First, let's look at the cards you've got out," Nick said. "You guys all got clean hands?"

No one bothered to answer him; he'd seen them wash their hands moments before. Small Dog started. "My first one's a Mickey . . ." He paused, letting the name sink in. Albert watched everyone's eyes shift to him, anticipating the next word. A Mickey Mantle could be worth hundreds. "Lolich," Small Dog said, smiling at his little joke. "Nineteen sixty-seven."

Nick frowned and scanned his catalog. "Two dollars," he said. "Next?"

They continued, moving as fast as Albert could write. Every card was worth something; some only a dollar, a lot of others between five and ten, and every once in a while one would surface that would be over ten. When they were halfway through, Yuno proudly announced a 1970 Roberto Clemente that Nick valued at thirty-two dollars minimum, without looking in his book. Everyone got up to admire it. Albert took a look to confirm that such a card really existed.

They went through more and more cards until Albert's writing hand was cramped. Princess held up the final one. "Nellie Fox, nineteen sixty-five."

"Six dollars, minimum." Nick looked up from his book. "That it? For the ones we got out, anyway?"

"That's it," Small Dog said.

"What's it look like so far, Alibi?" Nick asked.

Albert finished adding. "Three hundred seventy-eight cards." He waited, holding back on the number everyone wanted to hear.

He heard nothing but the drone of a fly somewhere in the room. "For a total of roughly $2,247.50."

Princess let out a long, low whistle. Small Dog said, "Yes!" The rest of them sat with open mouths turning up into smiles.

"Roughly?" Nick asked.

"I added it up in a hurry," Albert said, "but it's real close."

Princess took a breath. "Over four hundred dollars each."

Nick eyed his book. "And that's minimum."

"For twelve seventy-five," said Albert.

Yuno sat on the floor, pushing aside the wrapping. "And we still, you know, have something else in here."

All eyes were on him while he separated a box from the paper. Princess and Nick hovered over Yuno, peering anxiously at a small tackle box.

"It doesn't feel very heavy," Yuno said, giving it a little shake.

"Careful," Nick said.

"They're cards, Sponge Brain," Albert said, "not your mother's best dishes."

"Open it, Yuno," Nick said.

Yuno pried the latches up and raised the lid. "Paper," he said. "Just paper." He pulled out some thin shreds of paper, letting them fall to the floor. Then some more. And some more. A small mountain of confetti formed between his feet.

"No cards?" Nick said, moving closer.

Yuno pulled away, one hand still groping through the paper shreds. "Wait," he said, and lifted something out. He dropped the tackle box on the floor and held up the object.

Albert stared at it. It was another box—he could see its little hinges and clasp—but a special kind of box. Roughly the size of a thin wallet, it was shiny gold, with designs etched into its surface.

"A cigarette case," Princess said, taking it from Yuno. "My grandfather had one. Got it from my grandmother, back when smoking was acceptable." He turned the case over, examining it slowly. "This is a rather fancy one."

"Can you open it?" Nick said. His right eyelid twitched as he stared at the gold box and moved closer to Princess. Albert found himself leaning toward them.

Princess pressed the clasp. It popped open with a small click. He removed a piece of paper from the case and gently unfolded it. Inside was a single card. He picked it up carefully, barely touching the edges. Princess didn't know baseball cards, but he knew this would be something special.

"Willie Mays," he said, turning over the card. "Nineteen fifty-one."

The color drained from Nick's face.

"Put it back, Princess," Nick said, just above a whisper. "Very carefully."

Princess did as he was told and placed the open case in Nick's outstretched hand. Nick wiped the other hand on his pants and lifted the card back out of its wrapping. Gently. By one edge. He looked at both sides, swallowed, and put it back in the case unwrapped.

"Everybody needs to see this, but don't touch." Nick handed the case to Albert and opened his catalog, hurrying through the pages.

Albert stared at the card. He'd heard of Willie Mays, but couldn't remember seeing his picture before. Except for the old-fashioned uniform, there really wasn't much to set this card apart from a lot of others.

"I knew it," Nick said, studying his catalog. "It's his

rookie card. It's Willie Mays's rookie card."

Albert waited for him to go on, but he just stood there, grinning and shaking his head.

"So what's that mean?" Small Dog said as Albert handed him the case.

"It means we got lucky, once-in-a-lifetime lucky." Nick looked at them, an awestruck grin on his face. "It's worth thirty-eight hundred dollars. At least thirty-eight hundred. But probably more than four thousand, in this condition. It's perfect."

"Eight hundred for each of us," Princess said.

Nick glared at him. "*If* we were going to sell it."

"Why wouldn't we?" Princess asked, but Albert could see the answer coming.

"Sell a Willie Mays rookie card?" Nick said. "*Sell a Willie Mays rookie card?* A once-in-a-lifetime card, and you want to sell it?" He frowned and shook his head. "You sure you're not from another *planet,* Princess?"

"How else would we get our money?" Albert asked. "If we don't sell the card, what happens to it?"

"We'll just keep it," Nick said.

"Who'll keep it?" Small Dog said. "In a few months, we won't even be livin' here. We might not even see each other. Then what?"

Nick didn't have an answer, but he looked as if he was searching for one. His eyes darted from face to face, finally focusing on the ceiling. Albert looked up, half-expecting to see some inspirational words written there in gold letters.

"I'd pay you for it," Nick said.

Everyone laughed. Everyone but Nick.

"With what?" Albert asked. He'd seen Nick spend money; he'd never seen him save any.

"I could get a job. A paper route or something."

"And pay us off in about five years," Small Dog said. "If we're lucky. No, thanks."

Nick looked desperate. And then his frown disappeared, reshaping itself into a grin.

"How about a contest?" he asked. "We could have a contest, and the winner would get the card."

"What kind of contest?" But Albert had the answer to his question before Nick opened his mouth. Nick was a year older, a year bigger, and the athlete of the group. There wasn't a sport that anyone else could do as well.

"Oh, I don't know." Nick walked across the room and picked up Small Dog's basketball. "A little one-on-one tournament, maybe. Or H-O-R-S-E." He put his hand on a soccer ball. "We could do penalty kicks. Or kick for distance. Or have a juggling contest." Nobody even twitched. "We could do something in football. Or baseball. Or track. Or swimming. Whatever you guys want."

"How about if we *give* you the card?" Yuno asked.

"That would be just as fair."

"We could have a speed-reading contest," Albert said, only half-joking. But his suggestion got the same blank stares Nick's had.

Small Dog grinned. "Calf-ropin'." His suggestion got some laughs.

"Let's just draw names from a cap," Princess proposed. "It would be fair. And quick."

Nick gave Princess his you-must-be-from-Mars stare again. "A Willie Mays rookie card." He shook his head. "And you want to decide who gets it by pulling a name from a stupid cap?"

"Better than your ideas," Albert said.

"Yeah," Yuno said, and everyone but Nick echoed him.

"I haven't heard any that I liked," Nick said. "You guys got any better ones?"

For a long moment nobody said anything.

"Sell it," Princess said. "I still say, sell it. That way everyone would get something."

"Money." Nick spat out the word. "That's all we'd get."

"That's enough for me," said Small Dog.

"But wouldn't you rather have a lot of money?" Nick asked. "If I got the card, I'd never sell it, but think of what you could do with four thousand dollars."

Nick had made his point, and it was a good one.

Albert thought of some things he could buy with that money. He pictured himself cruising down the highway in a shiny green sports car, coming up behind a big lumbering logging truck and blowing by it so fast that its mudflaps spun around like pinwheels.

"It would have to be a fair contest," said Princess.

"Not any, you know, sports stuff."

"That doesn't leave much," Nick said.

Albert looked at his watch. "We don't have to decide today. Why don't we let Nick keep the cards overnight? We know he'll take good care of them. Tomorrow we can divide up the regular ones. By then maybe we'll have some ideas."

Nick shrugged his shoulders. "Sounds okay to me, Alibi."

Everyone else agreed to the plan, and a few minutes later the cards and list were neatly stored in the tackle box, which Nick hoisted two-handed to his hip. "How about two o'clock tomorrow at my apartment?" he said. "My parents will both be gone."

As they filed out of Small Dog's apartment, Albert checked his watch again.

"Shoot some hoops in a few minutes?" Nick asked.

"No, thanks," Albert said. "Maybe later."

"You got a date with some books?"

"Maybe."

"You gonna tell her?"

"Who?" Albert knew who Nick was talking about, but he needed some time to think about his answer.

"Maggie. You gonna tell Maggie what the cards are worth? You gonna tell her about Willie Mays?"

Nick really wasn't a sponge brain after all. He'd figured out Albert's plans as quickly as Albert himself had.

Albert nodded. There wasn't any point in lying to him. "I think I better," he said. He flinched, half-expecting Nick to turn red and explode.

But it didn't happen. Instead, Nick studied Albert's face. "You do what you have to do. If she wants the cards back, you know where to find 'em." He headed for his apartment.

Albert watched him go, deciding that he hadn't really known Nick very well, until today. He wondered if there were any more surprises still to come. He got on his bike and pedaled away from the apartments. The sun was still well above the trees. He had plenty of time for a talk with Maggie.

❖ FIVE ❖

Dinner was cooking by the time Albert got home. His mom was sitting on the sofa reading the paper. She looked up and smiled as he hurried by on his way to the bathroom. He closed the door behind him, found her hand mirror, and examined the back of his head in the wall mirror. His hair covered up the knot. His neck looked a little red, but he could say he scraped it on a branch or something. That was kind of true. He went back to the living room.

"A little late, aren't you, Albie?" his mom said.

"We found a garage sale." The lure of a garage sale was one thing his mom appreciated.

"Get anything?" she asked.

"Books." He patted the paper bag under his arm. "*The Lord of the Rings* trilogy, plus *The Hobbit*. And one by Maggie Heller, a local author who writes kids' books. And *The Adventures of Huckleberry Finn*—an old one." He took *Huckleberry Finn* carefully out of the bag and held it up for his mom to see. The red cover looked dark and rich with the light from the lamp shining off its gold lettering. But he was most excited about Maggie's book. He hadn't even known she was a writer.

She'd given him an autographed copy of her new book, *In the Long Run.*

"Quite a find," his mom said. "Did you buy them from anybody I know?"

"The author," he said. "Maggie. I don't think you know her."

His mom shook her head.

When Albert had told Maggie about the cards— about Willie Mays—she didn't even blink. She smiled this kind of sly smile that told him she'd known all along. "What are you guys going to do with them?" she asked.

"Divide them up," Albert said, "except for Willie Mays. Nick doesn't want to sell it. So we've got to figure out something."

"I think he's right," she said. "It would be a shame to sell that one."

"Right," Albert said, but he was surprised that she thought so. She hadn't seemed to be on the same wavelength as Nick. "Got any ideas?"

But she didn't have any. So he'd headed for home, with a small detour to tell Nick that everything was okay. Old Sponge Brain had greeted the news as if it were an extra December twenty-fifth. But he hadn't come up with any good ideas, either, and none of the other guys had called him.

Albert said hi to his dad and took his books to his

room. Within a couple of minutes he was back standing next to his mom, ready for his nightly predinner reading time, waiting for part of the paper. Without looking up, she handed him the first section. He plopped down on the floor.

An article on page five got his attention. Under a headline that read, "Vets Meet Here to Continue Last Man Tradition," was a picture of five old guys posing on the deck of a ferry. The story said that the last survivors of the crew of a World War II submarine had formed a last man's club, setting aside a German helmet, a case of French wine, and $5,000. Now they were down to five men, and the money had grown to more than $90,000. One of the old men said the only problem was that by the time everyone else was dead, the one who was left would be too old to enjoy the money, and there wouldn't be anyone left to drink the wine with. "The helmet might come in handy, though," he said. "I expect that I'll be falling down a lot by then." Albert smiled. If he didn't start wearing a helmet himself, he might not live that long.

"Dinner!" his dad called. Albert jumped up and headed for the kitchen.

Then it hit him. He asked himself why it wouldn't work, and he couldn't think of any reason. SoftEdge was paying for its employees to live in these tiny apartments temporarily—until they found permanent housing—so they'd all be gone before long. But no one knew exactly when anyone would be moving. And someone would have to be last.

"Excuse me a minute." He headed for his room before anyone could object.

Nick said hello on the second ring.

"A last man's club," Albert said.

For a long moment, there was silence on the line. "Alibi?" Nick said finally.

"We could have our own last man's club."

"Uh-huh. What's a last man's club?"

"Look in the paper. Page five. We could do like those old guys. Except the last one of us left at the apartments will get the card."

"Hold on."

Albert heard Nick drop the phone. A minute later he was back, rustling through the paper. "Found it," he said.

"Read it. I'll call you back as soon as I'm done with dinner." Albert hung up and headed for the kitchen. He needed a specific plan for how it would work. He knew that if Nick liked the idea, he'd definitely have his own version.

Albert was chewing his last bite of pizza when the phone rang. Mr. Patience must have had a hard time waiting. Albert decided to answer it in his room.

"I like it," Nick said.

"You do?"

"Don't *you?* I mean, I guess you must, since you came up with the idea. But I don't see why anyone won't like it, unless their parents have already found a place, and I don't think anyone has."

"You think it's fair?"

"Yeah," Nick said. "Probably too fair. I was kind of looking for an advantage."

"I noticed."

"It's a Willie Mays, Alibi."

"So where do we go from here?"

"Find out what the other guys think at the meeting tomorrow, I guess. If they go for it, we'll have to decide how to do it, exactly."

"Yeah," Albert said.

"One thing I thought about," Nick said, "is that we need to find someplace to keep the card until somebody wins it."

Albert hadn't seen that as a problem. "Can't you just keep it at your place?"

"What if some burglar breaks in and finds it? It wouldn't be the first time one of these apartments has been robbed. It happened before you moved in— three places got hit—and they took everything worth taking."

"In Granite Falls?" Albert looked up at his window—his fragile, ground-level window, and had no trouble picturing a thief coming through it. It would be too easy.

"In Granite Falls. Besides, my mom believes in regular room inspections, and she can sniff out a foreign object before she even walks in the door. I don't want to have to explain to her what's in the box."

"Your mom isn't the only snoop," Albert said. "My parents are the same way. In fact, I can't think of anyone's apartment where the card would really be safe."

"So where can we keep it?" Nick asked. "A safety deposit box—at a bank?"

"I wonder if you can do that. I wonder if they even let kids get one."

"Sounds kind of complicated."

"Yeah," Albert said.

"We need to think of something else."

"Come on over."

"Be there in a minute," Nick said, and hung up.

SIX

Albert switched on his TV as Nick plopped down on the big beanbag chair in the corner of the bedroom. Albert figured the noise would drown out their conversation before it got through the door.

Albert sat down on the bed. "Any ideas?" he said. So far, he'd drawn a blank—the ache in his head and neck and back wasn't helping—and he realized he'd been counting on Nick to come up with something.

But Nick just shook his head. "Not yet." He popped a chunk of black licorice in his mouth and glanced at the small bookcase by Albert's bed. "Any of those books have anything in 'em?"

Albert leaned over and scanned through the titles, recalling the stories. He was sure he'd never read a book about baseball cards, but what about something else, some kind of treasure?

He thought of *Treasure Island* and other pirate stories he'd read. What had the pirates used for hiding places? As far as he could remember, they'd all buried their treasure chests in some out-of-the-way place, and then made a map.

"We could bury it—the box and everything!" Albert

said. "Hide it in some spot where nobody would ever find it. Maybe the river—the pool. Nobody but us ever goes there."

"Not a bad idea, Alibi," Nick said absent-mindedly. He was leaning forward, chewing mechanically, intent on the television.

Albert caught a whiff of licorice. He wasn't sure how Nick could stomach the stuff. "Sponge Brain? You hear me?"

"Look at this, Alibi."

On the TV screen, a trio of cowboys was rolling back a phony-looking boulder from the entrance to a cave. The background music grew louder as one of them picked up a torch that was conveniently lying at the side of the entrance, and lit it. The camera focused on their faces, grim and full of resolve.

In an instant Albert realized what Nick was thinking, and his insides rose and fell, as if he'd just gone over the edge on a roller coaster.

"It's not a good place."

He didn't like the sound of his voice—a weak-throated whine.

"It'll be perfect," Nick said, as if it had already been decided. "It's far from here—far from everything—and nobody knows about it except you and me. It's the safest place we'll find."

Albert heard the words, but he wasn't really

listening. He was trying to come up with an argument that would keep Nick from going to the other guys with this idea.

But all he could think about was the old mine, and the day he and Nick had discovered it. It still gave him shivers, even in the early-evening warmth of his bedroom.

"What if somebody else finds the card?" he asked finally.

"Who? Nobody'd been there in years before we found it. Remember the spider webs, Alibi?"

Albert remembered them all right, clinging like foul gray cotton candy to the entrance and walls of the mine.

"It's a long way from the highway, off the trail, and hidden by bushes and trees and stuff," Nick said. "Even if somebody found the mine and went in, they wouldn't find the card; we'll bury it somewhere inside." He grinned. "We'll put it on the other side of the crevasse."

The crevasse. Albert had tried to forget about it. It was no big deal to Nick. He'd made it across—easily. All Albert remembered was how wide it was, how deep. And at the bottom, the dark, cold rush of water.

"Now all we have to do is figure out when to take it there," Nick said. "And come up with some rules. And a way to keep somebody from telling where it is, or going back and getting it on their own." Nick had his mind made up.

"We'll have to make a plan," Albert said finally. He grabbed a pad of paper and a pen from his desk and wrote "Last Man's Club" on top of the first sheet.

"I'm ready for ideas," he said, but his mind was stuck on one unpleasant idea: the mine.

SEVEN

Albert trudged around another turn. Through the boughs overhanging the deer path, he saw the clearing, and the steep, gray face of the mountain. From here, he could have hit it with a stone. And why shouldn't he? He could feel it mocking him.

The pile of rocks at its base looked the same as last time—as tall and wide as a small house, framed by trees and bushes that had survived the avalanche or grown up around it. Nick, Small Dog, and Princess were already there. Nick stood with his back to the rock slide, not even breathing hard. Small Dog and Princess leaned against thick-trunked fir trees, catching their breath. And as Albert stopped walking, rubber-legged and light-headed, Yuno staggered past him and sank to the ground. He stretched out flat on his back, staring at the sky. Albert felt like joining him, but he wasn't about to admit that he was a wimp. They'd find that out soon enough. He forced his legs to move again, propelling him aimlessly around the small clearing. Hands on hips, bent over at the waist, he slowly recovered from the trip up the steep trail.

They'd left their bikes hidden at the trailhead and negotiated a mile of switchbacks through thick forest and dense undergrowth, of rushing streams and detours. At last they'd come to the spot where, back in June, he and Nick had followed the deer. They'd lost the deer, but their search had led them to the mine.

The sounds of lungs sucking air were interrupted by Small Dog's voice. "How much farther?"

"We're here," Nick said.

That got everyone's attention. Even Yuno propped himself up on one elbow. "Where? Where's the, you know, hiding place?"

"We'll show you," Albert said. "You ready, Sponge?"

"Ready."

"Okay, everybody up," Albert said.

They formed a ragged circle. "Everybody happy with the cards they got today?" Nick asked.

Nobody said no. Albert would've been surprised if someone had complained. They'd decided at yesterday's meeting to split up the cards fair and square—rounds of picks, just like a regular sports draft. And there were enough good cards that nobody got shortchanged. Only one card stood out from all the others.

"Let's go." Nick turned toward the rock pile.

They angled off to the right and reached the shadows of the small canyon formed by the cliff face and the pile of rocks.

Albert felt the cool air from the mine before he saw the entrance. They stopped only a few feet away, but it was still hidden by rocks and vegetation. A chill crept down his sweaty back.

Nick shrugged off his backpack, pulled out two flashlights, and tossed one to Albert. "This is it, guys," Nick said. "Watch your heads on the way in."

Albert wasn't ready, but his feet moved anyway. Nick took a few steps and disappeared between clumps of thick bushes. The rest followed, with Albert bringing up the rear. The chill grabbed him. He tottered onto the rocks and smelled the familiar odor of damp rot.

The mine entrance was a rectangular black scar against the base of the cliff wall. The rock slide had left just enough room to get inside. Albert had been hoping that there'd been another slide, big enough to wipe everything out, but he wasn't surprised that it hadn't happened. He guessed that these rocks had come down a long time ago.

Albert watched Nick duck his head and disappear into the mine, followed by the others. Yuno stumbled through the entrance, his head barely clearing the old timber. Wispy, gray webs stretched across the top of the opening. Albert was only a step away now, but he still couldn't see inside, and he couldn't hear any voices. What he did hear gave him a chill: the rush of running water—fast, deep, running water. Even in the driest season of the year, the river was still flowing. He took a breath, checked his flashlight, and stepped in.

❖ EIGHT ❖

Just inside the entrance, the rock pile dropped off—faster than Albert remembered—and he lost his balance, lurching forward. He skidded to a halt in the middle of the rest of the guys, who were waiting for him in the dim light from the doorway. Albert looked back; the dust he'd stirred up billowed into the air, rising like thin smoke in the shaft of sunlight.

"Have a nice trip, Alibi?" Nick said. Someone giggled nervously, but no one else made a sound. Albert ignored the question and shone his flashlight toward the back of the mine. The crevasse wasn't hard to find—a black wall-to-wall gash in the floor. He let the beam rest there for a moment before he started past the others and into the gloom.

Nick clicked on his flashlight and followed. Yuno stood like a statue, his features frozen. Albert looked back. "Come on, Yuno. It's not that bad." But it *was* that bad, and Albert could feel his skin get cold from the inside out. Why had he agreed to go along with Nick's plan?

Nick's light stopped moving. A moment later it flashed back and forth across the width of the mine— a distance of maybe fifteen feet. He let the light play along the edge of the crevasse. The rush of the water grew louder as Albert inched toward the edge and peered down, his flashlight beam searching for the bottom. He glimpsed black water and white froth. Something touched him on the shoulder. Albert jumped back and landed in a crouch three feet from the edge.

"It's just me," Yuno said.

"Don't do that!" Albert looked around to see if anyone else had seen him jump. In the dark, it was hard to make out any expressions, even with two flashlights on. The inky surfaces of the mine seemed to swallow the light, and the sunlight barely penetrated this far.

"If you've got another one of those jumps in you, you won't have any trouble clearing the hole, Alibi," Nick said.

"Clearing the hole?" Yuno said. "You mean we've got to, you know, jump over this hole?" He edged closer, staring down into the blackness. "No way. That's gotta be ten feet across. Isn't there a log or something we could use?"

Albert figured the distance was more like eight, but it seemed like twenty-eight.

"There's a timber," Nick said, "if you think you need it."

"Doesn't look very far," Princess said. "We can have a go at it."

"Don't look too bad to me," Small Dog said. "I've jumped wider creeks than this."

"It's not a creek," Yuno said. "It's more like the Grand Canyon. That's a real river down there."

"Looks like eight or nine feet," Small Dog said. "I've done eleven."

"Yeah," Nick said, "but this time there's no dog chasing you."

Everyone but Small Dog laughed.

"Me first," Nick said. "Give me some light, will you, Alibi?" He backed away, allowing himself thirty feet to run at it. Without hesitating, he took off.

Albert kept his flashlight aimed at the far edge, showing Nick his landing spot. Nick approached the hole, rocketed off the ground, and floated through the air. He grunted as he landed on the other side, easily clearing the edge. Albert wasn't surprised; he'd seen Nick jump the crevasse with only a glimmer of gray light to mark it. Albert heard a low chuckle, and then Nick's flashlight was pointing back across. "Next?" Nick said.

For a moment no one moved.

"I'll work the flashlight over here." Albert's words felt shaky coming out. He didn't know if anyone could tell how scared he was.

"I'll be next," Princess said. Albert kept his flashlight beamed on the edge. His turn was coming, and he wasn't ready. He was never going to be ready. He would always just be a jellyfish. And who'd ever heard of a jellyfish jumping over anything?

Princess sprinted toward the hole, quick and light-footed, and jumped—too early! Albert thought. But he landed solidly on the far side.

For a long moment the only sounds came from the other side—from Nick and Princess—where the mood was one of celebration. Albert's side was quiet.

Finally, Small Dog spoke up. "I'll go," he said. He walked slowly toward the entrance and stopped, turning back to the hole. Against the light, Albert could see his shoulders rise with a deep breath. He lowered his head and took off, digging for the flashlight beam.

Halfway to the hole he stumbled. He regained his footing and accelerated, but he'd lost some speed, and his leap barely carried him to the other side. His left foot slipped, sending a shower of gravel into the water below. Albert's heart climbed into his throat. He watched Small Dog teeter on the edge before scrambling to safety and collapsing on the floor.

Again, sounds of elation rose from the other side.

In a moment, the voices died, leaving only the rush of water.

"Next?" Nick said, and someone laughed—someone from the other side. "You guys coming?"

"I'm not gonna do it," Yuno said. "I'm just gonna, you know, watch."

"Figures," Nick said. "Alibi? Are you coming?"

Albert inched forward, peering into the hole. It looked like an abyss—wide and deep and dark and dangerous—and he knew he couldn't make it. He knew he'd end up at the bottom, in a cold underground river going who-knows-where. He could barely talk. "No," he managed. "I can't do it."

Someone laughed again—Small Dog, Albert figured, half-wishing he had gone off the edge—and Yuno said, "Shut up, Small Dog. You're lucky you're not a corpse."

Nick laughed. "That's telling him, Yuno. Why don't you and Yuno get the timber, Alibi? We all need to be over here for this."

The timber. Albert flashed his light against the wall and spotted it, lying right where he and Nick had left it. "Come on, Yuno," he said softly. "This is how I got across last time." He led Yuno to the big wooden beam, and together they dragged it to the hole. It was close to twenty feet long, a foot wide, and more than half a foot thick, but not nearly as heavy as it must have been seventy or eighty years ago, Albert decided. Time had dried it out, made it light enough so he and Yuno could lift and pull and shove one end of it farther and farther over the chasm. When it touched the other side, Nick, Princess, and Small Dog dragged it onto solid footing.

"Go ahead, Yuno," Albert said. "It's sturdy." He tossed his flashlight to Princess, who pointed it back across. Yuno got on the timber in a crouch, looking straight ahead, hands and feet glued to the narrow bridge. Nick's flashlight lit up the other side. Slowly, Yuno moved along, half-duckwalking, half-crawling.

Albert followed, not really scared anymore— he'd done this before. He couldn't see the other guys' faces in the dark, and he wasn't taking his eyes off the beam, anyway, but he knew they were smiling, at least inside—smiling while he and Yuno crept across the crevasse, clinging to the timber like babies to their mother.

Albert felt the chill rising from below him and looked down. He was halfway across the beam now, inching along, wondering when the floor of the mine had caved in. Had it been long, long ago, when men still worked this mountain for silver and gold? Had the floor collapsed suddenly, taking men with it—men with wives and children back in some little town or camp? Or maybe it had happened just a few months or weeks or days before he and Nick had been up here last time. Maybe it wasn't done yet. The floor looked solid, but what if it was just a thin shell with nothing under- neath except black space and deep water?

Albert took his time; maybe he could still preserve a little dignity. When he finally hopped off the beam,

Princess handed him his flashlight. They all turned their backs on the river and made their way farther into the mine.

"Okay, everybody, get into a circle." Nick stopped in a wide section of the passageway. "Everyone but Alibi take off your shirt."

Albert heard some grumbling, but a circle of shirtless bodies formed.

"It's time for your speech, Alibi," Nick murmured under his breath.

Albert straightened up. He cleared his throat. "In the old days," he began, "men would seal an agreement and swear themselves to secrecy by the drawing and mixing of their blood."

Three quick protests filled the mine.

"We're not going to do that. Instead, I'm going to take off my sweatshirt and pass it around the circle for everyone to put on."

More protests.

"Twice. So everyone's sweat gets shared." Albert removed the shirt and started it to his left, to Nick, who put it on gingerly, whipped it off, and passed it on. It moved around the circle and back to Albert. And then a second time around. Its progress was marked by groans of disgust.

"Now repeat after me," Albert said when the shirt returned to his hands. "I vow to keep this endeavor a secret from all outsiders and never attempt to recover the bounty by dishonesty, trickery, or stealth."

Albert repeated the vow in short phrases. The other guys echoed them back.

"Now I'll go over the rules again while we look for a spot to bury the box."

Nick pulled the small tackle box and two dry T-shirts from his backpack. He tossed one of the shirts to Albert.

"The box stays where we bury it," Albert said, "until there's only one of us left living at the apartments. Then that guy—the last man—can come back and dig it up. Until then, no one comes back. And no one talks about it. Any questions?"

There weren't any. "You got a place?" Albert asked Nick.

"Over there." Nick pointed his flashlight at the base of the wall. "A soft spot. Nice and dry and out-of-the-way."

Nick used a flat rock to scrape out a foot-deep hole in the dirt and gravel. Albert wrapped the box in the sweatshirt and placed it in the bottom of the hole. Nick covered it back up, smoothing and shaping the top layer until it looked exactly like the surrounding floor. He picked up a big football-shaped rock, took two paces along the wall, and put the rock down next to his foot. "Whoever the last man is," he said, "just remember that the box is buried two paces past the rock. It should be easy to find."

Albert had his own ideas about who the last man should be. All the way up here, he'd been thinking about that little sports car. He just had to bank his money for the next few years and collect interest on it. It would give him a nice start.

"How am I gonna, you know, get back over here to get it?" Yuno asked.

Nick laughed, and was joined by everyone else— everyone but Albert, that is. He'd had the same thought himself. "If you're the last man," Nick said, "you'll have to work that out yourself. Maybe you can talk Alibi into coming back up and helping you."

Not likely. Albert didn't plan on hanging around with Yuno after one of them moved. Yuno was an okay guy, but not exactly someone you'd choose to have for a friend.

They headed back toward the entrance. This time Nick didn't have anything to prove, but he couldn't resist showing off; he ran across the timber. Princess and Small Dog walked. Yuno and Albert crept across like cold toads and then dragged the timber back to its spot.

Albert breathed more easily when they reached the entrance and much more easily when they got outside in the sun. He'd survived. That was definitely something to be thankful for. But he'd also been humiliated, brought down lower than a snake—again.

The trip back was uneventful—slow and quiet and, for Albert at least, thoughtful. If he ended up as the last man, would he be brave enough to return by himself and claim the prize? More than anything, he wanted that baseball card. But he couldn't see himself slinking across the timber to get it. He pictured himself racing fearlessly toward the chasm, flying over the river, laughing with disdain when he landed easily on the other side. That was the way a Willie Mays rookie card should be claimed. Somehow he needed to come up with the courage and jumping ability to do it right.

The next day, he asked his dad if he'd ever done any long jumping, if he could give Albert some tips on how to practice. But his dad said he didn't know much about the sport—broad jumping, he called it. He suggested that Albert take up baseball, which had been his sport, or maybe read a book about broad jumping. But improving his baseball skills wasn't going to get Albert across the chasm. And he remembered once when he'd sent away for a book that would teach him karate in only thirty minutes a day. It didn't work. So he buried the idea about learning how to long jump, but not deep, and not forever. Just temporarily.

The rest of August passed quickly, without even a whisper of anyone's parents seriously looking for a house. Albert's mom and dad had talked to a real estate woman, but she hadn't come up with anything interesting. As for the rest of the guys, there was no news. The main thing on everyone's mind now—at least the one subject they would talk about—was school. Their summer routine was about to come to an abrupt end.

Albert's first day of school was a downpour of activity and confusion. It wasn't easy to find classrooms in an unfamiliar building where he knew just a handful of people. But he got to every class, sometimes before they started. And his teachers were mostly okay. His English teacher, Ms. Grommet, seemed to dislike poor posture and gum-chewing, but Albert kind of liked her. She was funny, and he liked teachers with a sense of humor. He also enjoyed the fact that the guy she chose as the gum-chewing sloucher was Small Dog, who got to stand tall with a wad of gum on his nose and read a fake account of how he'd spent his summer vacation.

Only one class had him worried—his P.E. class. And his teacher was someone he'd met before. Nick had warned Albert. Now Albert was going to find out himself about Mr. Rockwood.

The lock. The stupid lock was stuck. Again. And all around him lockers were flying open and spitting out clumps of ripe-smelling socks and sneakers and shorts.

Albert frantically twisted the knob. Sweat was trickling down his back. His breakfast inched up from his stomach.

He swallowed and tried again. He knew the combination, knew it in the dark, in his sleep. It was the sponge-brained lock that didn't know it.

And Mr. Rockwood was waiting in the gym for his first class of the day—his first victims—to arrive. Hoping that one would dare to be late.

And one was going to be late. Albert glanced around the locker room. Guys were slamming their lockers shut and hurrying for the door. Even Yuno, who measured time in days instead of minutes and hadn't figured out yet that he was supposed to be afraid of Mr. Rockwood, was dressed, picking something out of his shoe with a pencil. Then he got up from the bench and followed the rest of the class out, leaving Albert alone with his sweaty palms.

Albert tried the lock again, watching the gym door

out of the corner of his eye as it slowly closed. Patience this time. Slow and steady and accurate. Don't miss a number. Not even a little. Then pull. And it opened. *It opened.* He tore off his clothes, dressed in a blur, and headed for the door, his shirt on backwards, his shoes untied, his locker open.

When he sprinted into the gym, they were shoulder to shoulder in a long line. At parade rest. Mr. Rockwood stood at one end, his back to Albert, jawing at Yuno from a foot away. Maybe he hadn't noticed. Albert skidded to a stop at the other end, his heart pounding. For an instant it was the only sound he heard.

"Mr. Alger." The voice was a growl, low and mean. And suddenly he was there, toe to toe with Albert, peering down at him from his full height. He mirrored Albert's version of parade rest, bending forward slowly at the waist until his nose was six inches away from Albert's. His eyes narrowed above his grim mouth.

"Today is the third day of the school year, Mr. Alger," he rumbled. "The third day of this class. How many days have you been tardy?"

Albert didn't have to think long. "Three," he said. His voice came out in a squeak. Someone down the line snickered.

"Three?" Mr. Rockwood said as if he couldn't believe his ears. "Three? Three out of three? You shouldn't be tardy that often in an entire year, Mr. Alger. What's your reason?"

"My lock wouldn't open," Albert managed. "Again."

"Your lock wouldn't open? *Your lock wouldn't open?*"

Why did he always have to repeat himself? Albert swallowed. He could see the tiny blood vessels in Mr. Rockwood's eyes.

"Do you know the difference between a reason and an excuse, Mr. Alger?"

Albert shook his head. He figured he was about to learn.

"A broken leg, Mr. Alger," Mr. Rockwood said. "A heart attack. Rescuing a drowning child. A trip in the space shuttle. A call from the president. Your wedding. Your funeral. Those are reasons for tardiness, Mr. Alger."

The gym was as quiet as an empty igloo. And Albert felt cold.

"A sore leg, Mr. Alger. Heartburn. Rescuing a drowning poodle. A trip in a slow car. A call from the vice-president. Your brother's wedding. Your poodle's funeral. A stubborn lock. Those are excuses, Mr. Alger. And I don't accept excuses. You should have learned how to open that stubborn lock, Mr. Alger. Or replaced it. And you had better do one of those two things by tomorrow or there will be some consequences you won't appreciate."

Albert shrugged. What could this Mr. Robot do to him, anyway?

"Don't shrug your shoulders when I talk to you, Mr. Alger." His face was three inches from Albert's now. "Would you shrug your shoulders at your father?"

Albert thought he probably would. He thought he probably had. He shrugged. Or semi-shrugged. Halfway through it, he realized what he was doing. But it was too late.

Mr. Rockwood's face turned a deep shade of red. Albert cringed, waiting for the explosion. "And would your father take it, Mr. Alger? Would he simply grin at your lack of respect? If so, then he's not a parent. He's nothing but a glorified roommate."

Albert didn't remember ever hitting anyone, but he felt like it now. A quick, hard blast to the face—to the nose. Just a glimpse of blood before Mr. Rockwood retaliated and buried him. Who did he think he was to criticize Albert's dad? But Albert stood there, not saying anything, not moving his shoulders, not breathing. He just wanted Mr. Rockwood to go away—to become somebody else's nightmare.

"I understand you have a nickname, Mr. Alger. Is that correct?"

Albert nodded, wondering who had told him.

Mr. Rockwood stared down the line, daring anyone

to snicker. "What is it?" he asked.

Albert swallowed again. His throat was as dry as old bread. "Alibi," he whispered.

"Alibi?" Mr. Rockwood roared. "Alibi?" His mouth smiled, but his eyes didn't. "How appropriate." He straightened up, spun on his heel, and strode away, leaving Albert with an emptiness in his chest. Albert stared at the floor, afraid he was going to cry. But he wouldn't cry. This guy couldn't make him cry. No way.

When the whistle blasted to start them on their laps, he was wondering if Mr. Robot had ever had something go wrong, ever made a mistake, ever been late. And what kind of reason would he come up with?

Albert wanted to find out.

I t was nearly eight-thirty and dark when Albert stopped in front of the small white house. He'd had no trouble finding it. The address was in the phone book, and nothing was hard to find in Granite Falls.

He leaned the bike against the front hedge and crept to the driveway. Staying low, he scurried toward the car. He crouched behind it, his heart thumping, and felt in his pants pocket for the small screwdriver—the perfect tool, the perfect way to find out the difference between a reason and an excuse.

The front door was open to the warm September air, allowing dim light and the sound of Mr. Rockwood's voice to escape. At least it sounded like Mr. Rockwood's voice. But different, too. Low and growly, yes. But then high, light, childlike, as if he were talking to a baby. He must have company—somebody who would be keeping his attention away from the front yard.

Albert took a deep breath and let it out. He'd never done anything like this before, but someone needed to teach Mr. Rockwood a lesson. He didn't need to go around humiliating people, pretending he was

Mr. Perfect. And he'd have a hard time proving anything tomorrow. Nobody in the whole school liked him. Anybody would have enjoyed letting the air out of his tires.

Albert duckwalked to the left front tire and pulled the screwdriver from his pocket. It hung up on a fold in his shorts and jerked out of his hand, clanging to the pavement. Run, he told himself, but his legs wouldn't move; his heart felt frozen.

He waited, listening, but he heard nothing. Even in the house it was quiet now, and that sent a chill down his back.

Some kind of old-fashioned music started up. Albert breathed, feeling his heart beat again, loud and quick. He twisted off the tire's valve cap and picked up the screwdriver, suddenly wondering about fingerprints. But they wouldn't check them on this kind of crime—if it was a crime. He knew they wouldn't.

He pressed the flat side of the screwdriver blade against the valve. It spit out a sharp hiss. He pushed harder; the hiss grew louder as air rushed from the tire. He watched, fascinated, as the tire slowly pancaked against the pavement. When the rim had nearly reached the cement and the hiss was reduced to a feeble sputter, he pulled the screwdriver away and started for the left rear tire.

Something—a hand, but stronger than a hand—

held him back. The fingers pressed into the flesh of his shoulder, sending an icy signal down the nerves of his back. Go, the signal said. Get out of here. But it was too late. He wasn't going anywhere. And he knew who had him.

The voice was low, but not unpleasant—almost amused. "I would let you finish the others, Mr. Alger, but then you would be out here all night pumping them back up. Have you ever pumped up a car tire by hand, Mr. Alger?" Mr. Rockwood's fingers relaxed, retightening on Albert's shirt. He lifted Albert up and pivoted him around until he was standing, looking into the dark shadows of Mr. Rockwood's face. "It's a long, slow process, Mr. Alger."

All Albert could do was listen. Maybe if he listened really well, Mr. Rockwood would let him go.

"Do you think you're the first who's come here with revenge in mind, Mr. Alger?"

Albert kept his mouth shut.

Mr. Rockwood turned toward the house. "Don't move, Mr. Alger."

Albert stood in the dark, feeling chilled, feeling shamed. How could he have been so stupid?

In a moment, Mr. Rockwood was back. He handed Albert a pump, a flashlight, and an air gauge, and pointed at the tire. "Fill it up," he said. "Thirty-two pounds."

Albert began pumping while Mr. Rockwood watched, as close and dark as a shadow. Albert wasn't about to show Mr. Rockwood that he was a wimp. He'd spent all summer riding his bike up a mountain highway, and he was in good condition. Couldn't Mr. Rockwood see that?

Albert's arms were getting tired, but the tire was taking shape. He stopped and checked the air pressure: twenty-seven pounds. He began pumping again. His heart was booming and he was hot, but he tried to look relaxed and cool. A minute later he checked the pressure again: thirty-three pounds.

"Close enough," Mr. Rockwood said. "You may put the cap back on now."

The cap. Albert would have forgotten it. He replaced it and stood waiting. He had a feeling he wasn't finished.

"Faster than I would have guessed," Mr. Rockwood said. "I should have let you flatten all four and then put you to work. You got off too easily."

For a moment Albert's hopes rose. Maybe this was all he had to do. He waited, trying to see Mr. Rockwood's eyes as they looked into the darkness.

"What time do you get to school, Mr. Alger?"

"A quarter to eight, about."

"Seven."

"No, a quarter to eight. I don't get there much

before that. My first class—your class—isn't until eight o'clock."

"Seven, Mr. Alger. For the next two months. You'll be dressed and on the gym floor no later than seven-fifteen. Every day you're late will be another day added on at the end." Even in the dark, Albert could see the glint of his teeth and the spark from his eyes. "You are going to be my apprentice, Mr. Alger. And apprentices need to be early risers."

Albert's heart sank. "What will I tell my parents?"

"Tell them the truth, if you want, or you can give them an alibi. That's for you to worry about—on your way home."

Albert hurried to his bike. Suddenly a face appeared in the front window, as if it were floating in air. It was nearly expressionless as its dark, sunken eyes followed Mr. Rockwood's progress to the door. Above the face, a Mariners baseball cap rode, too big for a head that appeared shrunken and nearly bald.

The face drew back as Mr. Rockwood entered the house and closed the door behind him.

Albert stood frozen in his tracks, trying to guess at what he'd just seen. Whose face had it been?

The light went out in the front room, shutting down his thoughts. He checked his watch: after nine. He needed to go by the hardware store and get a new lock—one that worked. He turned at the next corner, pedaling toward the shopping center, wondering whether his parents would be missing him by now.

He didn't know what he was going to tell them. The truth? He didn't think so. He barely wanted to admit to himself what he'd done. He had to come up with some good story—yes, some alibi—and do it in a hurry. He only had until the next morning.

He found a lock—a big, sturdy one with a key—and hurried from the store. A key lock should be quick and sure; he had a neck chain to keep the key on.

His legs were weak and shaky when he got back on his bike, and he felt shaky inside, too. He wasn't supposed to be out this late on a school night. What if his parents asked him where he'd been? What if Nick or one of the other guys—one of the guys he was supposed to be with—had called, looking for him? Maybe his mom and dad would be distracted by work or something. They'd had a lot on their minds lately; that might be his only hope.

He concentrated. Block after block floated by, but he couldn't come up with anything, and now he could see the lights of the apartment ahead. Albert slowed, trying to give himself more time, knowing that he had no time to give. He had to get home.

He was going too slow. His bike was wobbling, and he was having trouble steering. Suddenly he felt dizzy. He stopped and planted his feet on the pavement, but the street was pitching and rolling like a wind-blown ocean. A car moving toward him stopped a hundred feet away, its headlights dancing up and down. In the black sky overhead, the moon swung back and forth like a pendulum between the treetops. But it was the treetops that were moving, and from the woods that lined each side of the highway, Albert heard a strange rustling sound, as if every leaf and needle and branch was stirring from a sleep.

Then it hit him: he was in the middle of an earthquake.

He pushed his bike to the center of the road, away from the trees, and leaned against it for support. A block away, sparks cascaded from a power line as a tree toppled against it, and a pole went down with a crash. The lights from the apartment buildings and every light up and down the road went out. Except for the moon and the lights from the one car, the night had gone black.

He closed his eyes, waiting for the end, for a tree or a power pole to come crashing down on him. He could smell the sharp, smoky perfume of burning wires.

And then it was over and everything was still—except his body. It was trembling, from the tips of his toes to the top of every standing-on-end hair on his head. He raised his hand high and watched its silhouette twitch and dance against the moon, like a spider descending from the charcoal sky.

He breathed and held the air in, hoping his lungs still worked. Slowly, through clenched teeth, he let the air back out. He started for home, pushing his bike toward the shoulder of the road, looking for downed wires. In front of him, the car crept ahead, moving toward him. As it passed, the driver, a young woman, rolled down her window. "Quite a ride, huh?" she said bravely, but her voice gave her away.

"Yeah." Albert was surprised he could even answer her.

"Need a lift?" she asked.

Albert shook his head; he felt too sick to talk.

"Okay, but be careful going that way. You'd be better off riding your bike than walking. I'm sure there are wires down back there."

"Thanks." Albert was going to be very careful. He'd heard somewhere that bad things came in threes; a killer log and an earthquake already added up to two. He watched the woman drive into the night. He got on his bike and pushed hard on the pedals, realizing that he hadn't thought about Mr. Rockwood since the earth started shaking. And even now his problem seemed a lot less important. He pedaled faster, heading for the dark apartment buildings less than a block away.

Albert turned in at the main entrance. Cars were idling in the driveways and parking lots of the complex with their headlights on, and knots of people were gathered around them, away from the buildings.

Albert headed for his building. The apartment was dark, but it looked okay. He pedaled slowly through the crowds, searching for his mom and dad.

"Albie!" He turned, realizing he was almost on top of his parents' car. Albert dropped his bike, and his parents grabbed him, crushing him between them. He hugged them back, wondering when they were going to ask him where he'd been.

But they didn't ask. And because school was closed the next day for a structural inspection, he had an extra day to come up with a reason for going in early. In the end, though, it wasn't much of a reason. "The P.E. teacher asked me to help him out for a few weeks," was what he said on the morning he went back. "That's nice," was what his dad said. His mom just smiled.

The earthquake had been the biggest one in the Puget Sound area since 1965. Damage to buildings, but no serious injuries. Albert wasn't exactly thrilled about it—he'd had nightmares for two nights in a row—but he couldn't complain about the timing.

That morning he was dressed and in the gym—still half-asleep—ten minutes before his scheduled time. But Mr. Rockwood was already there, doing push-ups in the middle of the floor.

"Mr. Alger," he said without breaking rhythm, "I see you're on time."

"Yes."

"The mop is in the corner, Mr. Alger. The floor—the entire floor—needs mopping. I want all the dust up. When you're through with that, there is debris in the locker room. Get rid of the debris. When you're done in there, you can inflate any of the balls that need inflating." He paused in the up position, looking at Albert from thirty feet away. "I know you can inflate things, Mr. Alger. I've seen you in action."

"Okay." Mr. Rockwood's humor wasn't getting any better, but at least he wasn't growling.

Albert pushed the big mop back and forth across the floor, watching Mr. Rockwood as he finished his push-ups and jogged to the chin-up bar mounted on the wall. Up and down he went, again and again, while Albert trudged back and forth like a zombie.

By the time Mr. Rockwood had finished his third or fourth set and jogged to the far end of the gym, Albert was nearly done with the floor. He watched as

Mr. Rockwood got down in a starting stance and sprinted to the other end of the gym and back. He stood, hands on hips, breathing hard for a few seconds, and went again, arms pumping, legs lifting, eyes—cool and distant—straight ahead. He was still racing up and down the gym floor when Albert leaned the mop against the wall and headed for the locker room.

The hour passed—not nearly as slowly as Albert thought it would—and he got on with his day. The next morning was the same. And the next. Mr. Rockwood went through his exercise ritual, stopping once or twice to check on Albert's progress. But Mr. Rockwood had no complaints, and after a few days he quit checking. Albert was getting everything done, and finishing it with time to spare. And while Mr. Rockwood wasn't exactly Mr. Congeniality, he wasn't quite as scary as he had been. By the middle of the second week, Albert decided to approach him with a proposition.

TWELVE

Albert had tried not to get his hopes up too high, but the goal was still there, in the back of his mind all the time: to be the last man.

One thing he knew was that he wasn't going back to the mine to inch across the beam like some slug. Next time, he was going to leap across, fly like a bat through the dark, musty air. And he knew someone who could show him how to do it.

It was Friday before Albert worked up enough courage to approach Mr. Rockwood. He did his chores as fast as he could without looking too obvious, and timed his exit from the locker room to the gym to coincide with Mr. Rockwood's last wind sprint. Albert crept up to him cautiously, as if he were approaching a hungry lion.

"What is it, Mr. Alger?" He was bent over at the waist, breathing deeply, but he straightened up. "Are you looking for more tasks?"

"No, sir," Albert managed.

"What is it, then? What do you plan to do for the rest of your time?"

"You know track, don't you, Mr. Rockwood?"

"Track?"

"Running and stuff. Jumping."

"Track and field."

"Yes."

"I was a decathlete, Mr. Alger. I've coached track and field for more years than you've been alive. I'd say I know a little about running and jumping." He gave Albert a half-grin, making him look half-friendly. "Are you interested in turning out in the spring? We might be able to find an event for you."

Turning out? Albert had never considered turning out for track. But if Mr. Rockwood thought he had some potential, maybe he should try. Albert wasn't sure about his speed, but he'd proved his endurance over the summer. "Maybe. I'd like to learn how to long-jump. Do you think you could show me how today, and I could practice here on the days I get done with my work early?"

"Today? Do you think I can teach you to long-jump in one day?"

"A few days, then," Albert said.

"Long jumping is an art, Mr. Alger—a difficult art. It can't be learned in a day or a few days. There are Olympians who are still searching for the perfect approach, the perfect foot placement, the perfect lift, the perfect flight, the perfect landing." He wet a finger on his lips and held it up, testing for the direction of an imaginary breeze. "The perfect wind behind their backs." He looked at Albert, as if trying to figure him out. "But we can get started. I'll teach you what I can, until your obligation is up here, or you lose interest."

"I won't lose interest."

"We'll see." Mr. Rockwood dragged a wrestling mat out of the equipment room and centered it under the basketball hoop. He pulled another one out; Albert helped him set it on the first one and line up the edges.

"Wait here." Mr. Rockwood motioned Albert to one side of the mats. He walked out past the half-court line and turned toward the basket. "The key to a successful long jump isn't length," he said in a voice that filled the gym. "At least, that isn't your immediate goal. Your immediate goal—what you're thinking about as you approach the takeoff board—is height." He got down in a semi-crouch, one foot in front of the other, and began rocking back and forth, his arms slowly pumping. "My takeoff point will be the free-throw line. What I'll be trying to do is fly high enough to touch the rim on my way by. Of course, I won't be able to do that. Very few humans can. But that is what I'm trying for. If I can get high enough, the distance will take care of itself."

He crouched lower, arms pumping faster, and took off. Albert watched him as he approached at full speed, planted his left foot on the line, and exploded into the air. He soared toward the backboard, legs moving, arms extended, and brushed the bottom of the net with his fingers. He landed on the edge of the mat in a crouch, nearly at the base of the wall. Albert let out a low whistle as Mr. Rockwood straightened up and turned back toward him, a frown on his face.

"Scratched. That one wouldn't count. I overstepped the takeoff mark. I guess I need some practice myself." He looked at the free-throw line, as if it were somehow to blame. "But you get the idea, don't you Mr. Alger? Sprint, plant, levitate, land. And don't foul. It's as simple—and as difficult—as that. Now you give it a try."

Mr. Rockwood stood off to the side, near the free-throw line. Albert took his position at half-court. He crouched, pumping his arms back and forth, and stared straight ahead, where he pictured a wide fissure in the floor. He could hear the roar of rushing water somewhere beyond its edge.

He breathed deeply, let it out, and took off, lifting his knees the way he'd seen Mr. Rockwood do. He could feel himself accelerating, but not fast enough, and now the line was coming up on him. He wasn't going to hit it right. He stutter-stepped, chopping his stride, and tried to accelerate again, but it was too late. The line was there, and he planted his left foot awkwardly, trying to lift off into the air. But there was no liftoff—just a clumsy low-level flight before he landed, barely making it to the mat. He stumbled forward a few feet before turning to see Mr. Rockwood chalk a spot on the mat. Albert calculated the distance from the mark to the free-throw line: seven or eight feet, maybe. No more than that. If he'd really been at the mine, he'd be in the water right now. The thought made him shudder. Mr. Rockwood looked at him curiously.

"Not far, Mr. Alger, but it's a starting point. You have nowhere to go but up."

Albert felt his face getting hot. "Pretty bad, huh?"

"A young man—even one without a lot of athletic ability—should be able to do close to his age," Mr. Rockwood said. "That's my rule of thumb. So if you're twelve years old—as I assume you are—you should be able to jump close to twelve feet. With training. With practice. Those are the keys."

He looked down at Albert's mark, and took two long strides back to the free-throw line. "Seven feet. Barely. That's the bad news. The good news is that you had no speed, you took off a half-foot behind the line, you got no liftoff, and you were staring at a spot buried under the floor somewhere out there. If you aim low, that's where you'll end up. Just as in life itself."

"Can I try again?" Albert asked.

"Again and again and again. That's the only way you'll improve. Think about what I've told you. Experiment until you find a starting point that will get you to the free-throw line without fouling or losing speed."

Albert took a position behind the half-court line again. He wasn't sure where he'd started last time, but this time he'd keep track. He put his locker key and neck chain on the floor next to his front foot, and began rocking back and forth, eyeing the free-throw line, and then the basket, and then the line again. How was he supposed to look at both? One at a time, he decided. But he found that even when he was concentrating on the line, he could still see the basket. He'd only have to change his focus once he got there.

He sprinted away, accelerated to the line, and jumped, staring at the basket as he left the floor. The jump felt better—more speed, more distance—but Mr. Rockwood didn't mark it.

"Scratched," he said. "Try again. Don't hold your breath on your approach. Stay loose. Once you're in the air, snap your feet back behind you so your body and legs form an L. When you're ready to land, pull your legs up and push them forward. It'll give you some extra distance."

Albert tried again, and scratched. On the next jump, his timing was off; he slowed up, took off like a blimp leaving the ground, and landed short of his first mark. But he kept trying.

A half-dozen jumps later, Albert was tired and frustrated; he still hadn't matched his first effort. A puny, wimpy effort, but he couldn't beat it.

"Try to imagine something you want very badly," Mr. Rockwood said, as Albert again took a spot behind the half-court line and moved the key and chain back six inches. "Then picture it sitting on the edge of the rim. All you need to do is get off a perfect jump, and you can snatch it away."

Albert didn't have to think hard about this one. He squinted his eyes, picturing the Willie Mays card perched on the front of the rim. He imagined a miniature Willie leaving the card, shagging down a long fly ball just before it hit the center-field wall.

Albert crouched, rocking back and forth, and glanced between the free-throw line and the rim before racing away, sprinting for the line. Willie was back from center field, and he was beckoning to Albert, asking him to come and get him, to jump high and far. He reached the line at full speed and pushed off. At the last instant, he brought his feet up and out, trying for more distance. He hit and bounced forward. He hadn't reached the rim, he hadn't come close, but he wondered how he'd done. The jump had felt better; it had felt good.

He turned to see Mr. Rockwood making a new mark on the mat.

"That was a good effort, Mr. Alger. It was a fair jump. You hit the line right, and you improved on your old mark by nine inches. Quite an improvement, but one you won't see every day. Some days you won't see any. Some days you'll go backwards." He pocketed the chalk and turned for the locker room. "If you can add a fraction of an inch a day, you'll be doing well. You have five more minutes. Get the mats put back. Then I'd suggest a series of ten sprints alternated with ten strides—if you're serious about this, that is."

"I am."

"Tomorrow I'll have a jump rope for you to use. You need to build up your legs."

Albert watched him walk to the locker room, head held high, back straight as a flagpole. He hadn't smiled today, but Albert had seen a little crack in the armor. Maybe there was some warmth in there after all. And Albert had learned more in fifteen minutes than he could have learned on his own in a month. Now all he had to do was keep the other guys from finding out what he was up to. He could imagine them laughing at him, saying he was wasting his time.

He got the mats put away and started his workout. He sprinted to one end and jogged back to the other. He wasn't sure what a stride was. He'd have to ask Mr. Rockwood. By the third time down the floor, he was breathing hard. He was on the seventh sprint when Yuno walked out of the locker room. Yuno, who'd never been on time for anything, was early.

THIRTEEN

For an instant, Albert thought about stopping the workout. But he'd still have an explanation to make, and he needed time to come up with something besides the truth. He wasn't proud of what he'd done at Mr. Rockwood's, or of getting caught. And he'd just as soon keep his reason for running sprints a secret, too; he didn't want Yuno hitchhiking on his idea. Albert had to think of something to tell Yuno, and he needed to do it fast.

Yuno walked toward the middle of the gym. He stood there, arms folded, while Albert cruised back and forth past him, concentrating on the backboards at either end.

Finally, Albert finished. He staggered to a stop and leaned against the wall, trying to catch his breath. Before he could, Yuno was there. "What did he, you know, get you for?" he asked.

Albert breathed a sigh of thanks. Yuno had given him his alibi—Mr. Rockwood was punishing him for something. But what? "He says I smart-mouthed him," he said.

"Tell him you're a smart guy," Yuno said.

"Oh, sure. And then I'd be here for the rest of the

year instead of just two months."

"*Two months?* What did you say to him?"

He couldn't come up with anything. "I'd rather not talk about it," he mumbled. "What are *you* doing here so early?"

Yuno got a funny look on his face and glanced over his shoulder. Finally, he shrugged and grinned. "I thought I'd, you know, come in for a little workout," he said. "I want to get in better shape—in case I get to be the last man and have to jump the stream."

Stream? It was a river. And Albert couldn't imagine Yuno jumping over it. But he didn't say that. "That's a good idea," he said. "Maybe I should do something like that, too. Just in case."

"Yeah," Yuno said, his face lighting up. "Maybe we could, you know, work out together. We could go to the track after school. There's a long-jump pit there and everything."

Training—or doing anything else—with Yuno wasn't in Albert's plans. "I don't think so," he said. "I'm going to be pretty busy after school. Lots of home-work and stuff."

"Okay," Yuno said. "Maybe if you ever have the time, we could."

"Maybe," Albert said.

Yuno looked up at the wall clock. "Gotta go." He took off on a slow jog around the gym. Albert thought he looked a little taller, or thinner—or maybe both. He was moving pretty well, but Albert wondered how long Yuno would stay interested in this exercise program. Albert gave him about a week.

But it wasn't a week—not even close. The next day Yuno came in at his regular time, tying his shoes and tucking in his shirt as he hurried to his spot. Albert smiled and decided that sleep—or breakfast—must have been higher on Yuno's priority list.

"What happened to your early workout schedule?" Albert asked him in the locker room after class.

"If Mr. Rockwood's gonna hand out big, ugly chunks of punishment, I'm gonna, you know, stay out of his way. My mouth sometimes gets me in trouble."

Yuno's plan had turned into a one-day flame-out. But Albert kept at his. He woke up in the mornings looking forward to improving his mark. After a week he'd added another three inches. Not much, but he could afford to be patient. So far, he hadn't heard a whisper about anyone moving. But he knew that it couldn't be much longer before that would change.

he first day of fall, a Saturday, felt more like summer—hot and still. Not house hunting weather. Albert got out of bed that morning and found his parents sitting at the kitchen table, drinking coffee—instant, probably.

"You guys want me to make you some eggs or something?" Albert asked.

"That would be nice, Albie," his mom said, looking up from her book.

"Scrambled?" Albert asked. "With grated cheese?"

"Yes," she said. "That's the kind."

"And some toast would be good, too, Albie," his dad said. He was going through a stack of papers from work.

"In the toaster, Dad? With butter?"

"That's the ticket."

"You want some of my special orange juice, too?"

"Hmm?" His dad was staring at a sheet of paper.

"You know. The frozen stuff in the can? With water?"

"That'd be great."

His dad's sense of humor seemed to be hiding under that stack of papers. And his mom was ignoring everything except her book.

"This is fascinating," she said, as if to excuse her lack of sociability. "Did you know that Eleanor Roosevelt practically ran the country during FDR's last two terms?"

"That book was written by a woman, wasn't it?" his dad said.

"That has nothing to do with the facts of the matter, Raymond."

"Of course not," his dad said. "And next she's going to write a book exposing the fact that Mrs. Shakespeare actually penned all of William's plays."

"You're impossible." His mom went back to her book. His dad grinned.

Albert decided to do some lobbying while their minds were partly elsewhere. "It sure is great living at the apartments, you know?"

They looked up at him with matching expressions. Quizzical. No, not just quizzical. More like, Who is this kid disguised as our son? A few weeks ago he'd been begging them to get serious about finding a house. Now this?

Albert started for the refrigerator. "I mean, we've got everything here. There's the swimming pool and the basketball court and the exercise room and Ping-Pong and the clubhouse. And no yard work for you, Dad. And I have lots of friends here now." He grabbed the food from the refrigerator without looking at his parents.

"Your friends won't be here much longer, Albie," his mom said.

"And I like yard work," his dad said.

"And this apartment is so small," his mom said. "There's no room for any of our things. Your dad's desk. My piano. We can't even get our books out of storage."

Albert couldn't argue with that one. He pulled a frying pan from the cupboard.

"There's not a lot of houses for sale right now," his dad said. "But as soon as the market improves, we'll be out looking again."

"Well, I'm not in a hurry." Albert figured maybe they hadn't gotten his point yet.

"That's good to know," his dad said. "I'm glad you've gotten more flexible since a while ago."

"When you were demanding that we move before school started," his mom said.

"Not exactly demanding, Mom."

"Begging? Pestering? Nagging?" She smiled.

"More like assertive whining," Albert said.

"Why the change of heart?" his dad asked.

Albert was ready for this one. The one question he'd been expecting. "Oh, I think I'm just starting to appreciate all we have here."

"I think you'll appreciate a new house even more," his dad said. "Now, how about that special breakfast?"

The conversation seemed to be over. Albert cracked an egg into a bowl and tossed the shell at the sink. He wondered if the other guys had tried this strategy yet.

He didn't ask. He just studied their faces every day, hoping he'd see some hint that things were going sour. But all he saw were poker faces staring back at him, looking for their own clues.

The end of September approached. And it had become an unspoken law that nobody mentioned the club. They saw each other every day, played, talked, argued, traded insults. But the subject of moving didn't come up. Even Albert and Nick didn't discuss it.

Until one Saturday morning when the phone rang, pulling Albert from his bed.

"Alibi?" the voice on the other end said. It was Nick. Wide awake and excited. Up to something.

"You got me out of bed, Sponge Brain."

"It'll be worth it."

"What will?"

"Come over as soon as you can. I've got something to show you."

"Ten minutes," Albert said. "But it better be good."

Nick chuckled in his ear and hung up.

Albert's curiosity was wide awake now. And five minutes later he was pressing Nick's doorbell, shifting from foot to foot, trying to ignore the empty ache in his stomach.

"You got anything to eat here?" he asked when Nick opened the door.

"Lots. My mom just went to the store." He was chewing licorice again. Albert had gotten used to seeing Nick's cheek ballooned out with a big black wad of the foul-smelling stuff. But not before breakfast.

"How can you eat that junk so early in the morning?" Albert said.

Nick ignored the question. "Thanks for taking a break from your book," he said.

"I wasn't reading a book," Albert said.

"Newspaper?" Nick said. "Magazine?"

"I was asleep."

"Sure, Alibi."

Albert spotted a pan of brownies on the kitchen counter. "These homemade?"

"Last night. Take one."

Albert took three, stuffing a whole one into his mouth.

"You hungry?" Nick asked.

"I told you, I just got up," Albert mumbled. "Why'd you call me, Sponge Brain?"

"I didn't call you Sponge Brain."

"Funny," Albert said. "Ha. Ha. Why'd you phone me, Sponge Brain?"

"I've got something to show you," Nick said.

In Nick's room, in his closet, sat a stack of magazines and papers. He picked them up and carried them to his desk. "Take a look at these," he said. A large, conspiratorial grin spread across his face.

Albert took the top magazine off the stack. *Home Market,* it was called. Under the name was a color picture of a beautiful big house on the water. Inside were more beautiful houses. And lots of regular ones.

He thumbed farther through the stack. More *Home Markets.* Then copies of a similar magazine called *Moving Up.* And packets of real estate information with a realtor's business card in each one. The name on the cards was Larry Borders.

"Who's Larry Borders?" Albert asked.

"My soccer coach," Nick said. "He's a real estate guy."

"Why'd he give this stuff to you?"

"I asked him for it. He had a bunch of it in his trunk."

"What I meant was, why'd you want it?" Albert said. "The last thing we need is a pile of real estate junk."

"You're not awake yet, are you, Alibi?" Nick said, shaking his head. "This stuff's not for us. Why do you think I have it hidden in my room?"

Albert thought for a moment. Maybe it was too

early for his brain to handle anything unusual. And then it hit him. "The other guys? Their parents?"

"You got it. I thought we needed something to get them going."

The possibilities raced through Albert's mind. "When?" he asked. "How?"

Nick pulled a stack of plastic grocery bags from his desk drawer. "I've had these for a while. Saved 'em for a special occasion."

"And?"

"We're going to put together twenty sets of this stuff and stick them in the bags along with one of the coach's cards."

"Then what?"

"Deliver 'em. Tomorrow morning."

"They'll know who brought them. The guys will figure it out."

"I don't think so. Nobody else knows who my coach is. And we're doing twenty sets. We'll leave seventeen of 'em with strangers. None will have kids in the club. Some probably won't even work for SoftEdge. We'll tell the guys that we each got a bag of stuff, too."

Albert smiled. Nick had this pretty well thought out. For a sponge brain. "Does your coach know you're doing this?" he asked.

"Yeah. I just told him I knew some people who were looking for houses."

"It might work," Albert said.

"It will."

They sorted and arranged and stacked and stuffed, until twenty bags of real estate literature were piled neatly in the corner of the closet. It hadn't taken them long. "I hope my coach is as good a salesman as he says he is," Nick said.

"I just hope someone calls him."

"No problem."

Albert wasn't so sure. But he found himself getting excited. It was going to be hard waiting until the next morning.

FIFTEEN

Albert's alarm chirped on at 4:30. But he was already awake, his hand poised above the clock. He touched the OFF button and swung his feet to the floor.

The apartment was quiet, asleep. The hallway and living room were dark, but he knew his way out. A moment later he was standing in front of Nick's apartment door. The cool morning air felt good on his face, relaxing him a bit.

Nick's door clicked open. "Grab some of those, Alibi," he whispered.

Nick stood there with an armload of bags, chewing licorice again. Albert could smell it. Another stack of bags sat on the floor. Albert scooped up the bags and stepped back outside with Nick right behind him.

They hit the club members' apartments first and then distributed the rest. They finished in ten minutes.

Too fast. Too easy. Albert had been ready for more excitement. But they were done. "Now what?" he asked, as they stood in the grass courtyard in front of the building.

"Back to bed, I guess. Get some sleep. Wait for the whining to start."

"I suppose you're right. As if we were never here."

"We weren't," Nick said. "Remember that."

"You too, Sponge Brain. See you later." Suddenly Albert felt tired.

But when he fell asleep, he dreamed. A dream of Nick, creeping back in the dark to Albert's door. With a giant grocery bag filled with real estate literature. And all the houses in all the brochures were big and beautiful. And cheap.

Albert woke in the dark. He knew it was a dream, but he had to make sure. He shuffled through the apartment to the living room.

He inched the door open, half-expecting to feel the weight of a huge plastic bag. But there was nothing there. And now he really needed to get some sleep. He closed the door and tiptoed back to his room. Two minutes later he was dreaming again.

The phone woke him. He picked it up, glancing at his radio. Eleven-fifteen.

"You heard from anyone yet?" Nick asked.

"No. Have you?" The cobwebs were starting to clear.

"Small Dog."

"What did he want?" Albert asked.

"Wanted to know if someone had left a bunch of real estate junk at my apartment. Said he'd found some spread all over his kitchen table. His mom told him someone had left it on their door."

Albert could hear the grin in Nick's voice. And he had to smile himself. "What did you tell him?"

"That the same thing happened to me."

"Why'd he call just you?"

"Not just me. He called Princess, too. Said the same thing happened to him."

"He didn't call me," Albert said. "Not yet, anyway. Did he say anything else?"

"He said something smelled."

"Something smelled? You think he knows any-thing?"

"How could he?"

"I don't know," Albert said. "I guess he couldn't."

"Anyway, it looks like it's working. Now we just have to hope for some action."

"Yeah," Albert said, without enthusiasm. "I'll see you later."

He hung up the phone and stood in the middle of the room, listening. His parents were gone and the apartment was quiet—still—like the eye of a hurricane.

He was hungry. He'd gotten dressed and started for the kitchen when he heard a pounding on the door. He hurried to the window and looked out. There they were—Small Dog, Princess, and Yuno. And they didn't look happy.

He stepped back and waited, hoping they'd pass

him by. But the doorbell rang. He eased the door open.

"Come on, Alibi," Small Dog said.

"Where?" Albert asked, grabbing onto the door jamb.

Small Dog looked at him curiously. "Nick's got some explaining to do."

Albert searched the other faces. All he saw was anger. He decided to keep a low profile. The mob swirled away, and he followed down the sidewalk, hanging at the back of the pack, keeping his mouth shut.

Nick had his door open before they got there. He stepped out on the sidewalk, an innocent smile on his face. "What's going on, guys?"

"Who's Larry Borders?" Small Dog asked.

Nick's smile froze. "I don't know. Some real estate guy, I guess."

He glanced at Albert, his eyes pleading for some help. But Albert didn't know what to say. How had they found out?

"Why are you asking me, Small Dog?" Nick asked, trying to thaw out his smile.

Small Dog held a bag out to Nick. "Is this the same kind of stuff you got?"

Nick took the bag and looked inside. "Yeah. Same stuff."

"Smell it," Small Dog said.

"What?"

"Smell the bag."

Nick held it up to his nose and took a careful whiff. Then a deeper one. "Licorice," he whispered.

"What?" Small Dog said. "We didn't hear you."

"It smells like licorice," Nick said. "The guy must've had licorice in the bag."

"All the bags," Small Dog said. "All the stuff in 'em."

Nick glanced quickly from Small Dog to Yuno to Princess, and finally to Albert.

"You're the only guy who likes black licorice, Nick," Yuno said, "who keeps a stash of it in a drawer so he won't, you know, run out."

Albert remembered now—the drawer where Nick had kept his giant supply of smelly licorice. The same drawer where he'd kept the bags. The amateur detectives had done a good job.

"Are you accusing me of giving out this stuff?" Nick asked, trying to sound indignant.

"Who else would have?" Yuno asked.

"I'm not the only one who eats licorice, Yuno," Nick said.

"Where's the stuff that was left on your door, Nick?" Small Dog asked.

Albert watched Nick's face flush. He could see him getting desperate.

"I . . . I . . . threw it away," Nick stammered.

"Where?" Princess's dark eyes flashed. "Show us where you threw it."

Nick's face got redder. He opened his mouth but no words came out. Finally, he held the palms of his hands out and shrugged his shoulders, forcing a smile. "It was just a joke, guys."

"I guess we'll see who ends up laughing." Small Dog started down the sidewalk with the others straggling behind him.

Albert let his breath out slowly, hanging back. He didn't know whether to follow them or stay with Nick: the sneak, the outcast, the leper.

Suddenly Small Dog turned around and stared at Albert as if a light had just gone on. "And what about you, Alibi?" he shot back. "You haven't said anything. Were you in on this with your buddy?"

Albert felt everyone's eyes on him. Should he deny everything, or share the blame with Nick, who was shaking his head "no," barely moving it from side to side.

Albert's first thought was how cool it was for Nick to stick up for him; his second thought was too slow in coming.

"No alibi this time, Alibi?" Princess said. "I guess we've got our answer then, don't we?"

"I guess so," Albert said. He knew he'd lost his

chance. "But it was just a joke."

"Just like that vow we all took in the mine?" Small Dog turned and started back up the sidewalk, joining the others, muttering something under his breath. Then they laughed. At least, two of them laughed. But Yuno glanced back at Albert with a look that Albert couldn't quite interpret. Hurt, maybe. Or disappointment.

Albert looked at Nick. He appeared smaller, as if someone had just let the air out of him. Albert wasn't feeling charitable. "Well, Sponge Brain, you really blew it this time."

"I couldn't smell anything. You should've told me."

"Every time I was around you, you were eating the nasty stuff. I thought the smell was just you."

"Well, I think I'm gonna give it up. No more licorice. This has to be some kind of omen or something."

"I think it's a little too late."

And it was. Two days later their parents started getting phone calls from real estate agents. And mail. And then agents were knocking on their doors. And leaving cards on their doorsteps. And calling them at work.

The Attack of the Real Estate People had begun.

O n the first Saturday in October, the club had its first casualty. Albert, Nick, and Small Dog were shooting baskets when Small Dog's parents drove up with his little sister in the back seat. At first Albert couldn't figure out why they'd parked there. But then he saw their faces—their crinkly-eyed, beaming faces.

"Your folks been house hunting, Small Dog?" he asked.

"Every day." Small Dog sounded disgusted. "Why?" His back was to the car.

"Look at their faces, Small Dog," Nick said, nodding in their direction. "It looks like they might have some good news for you."

Slowly Small Dog turned toward them, like someone hearing footsteps behind him in a dark alley. He frowned and pulled the ball close to his chest. His mom and dad stepped onto the court.

"Joey, we found a perfect—" Mrs. Zemo began.

"I don't wanna move!" Small Dog wailed.

"It's a great house, Joey," his dad said. "You're going to like it."

"I won't."

"We want you to come and see it," his mom said.

"I'm shooting baskets."

"Now," his dad growled, tapping his toe impatiently against the pavement.

Small Dog shrugged. He flipped the ball in Albert's direction and walked toward the car, his head down. His dad put his arm around his shoulders and walked with him. "You'll like it," he said.

Small Dog said nothing.

Albert watched them get into the car. He felt sorry for Small Dog. Or at least thought he should feel sorry for him. "Too bad. We'll miss him."

"Yeah. We'll miss old Small Dog. Kind of." Nick bowed his head respectfully before looking up. "Know who their real estate man is?"

Albert saw Nick's grin and knew. "Larry Borders?" He couldn't quite believe it.

"The one and only." Nick's grin was now spread across his whole face. "Not such a bad idea after all, huh?"

Albert ignored the question. He took a shot from the top of the key that missed the rim entirely. The ball banged off the backboard and bounced back to him.

"Admit it, Alibi. It was a good idea."

"He hasn't moved yet."

"You know he will," Nick said. "You saw the look on his parents' faces. They were in love—with a house. And as soon as they sign the papers, the company will pay for 'em to rent it until the deal's final. Small Dog could be out of here in a week."

That was true—Albert had heard his own parents talking about the program. He launched a shot from the free-throw line that rattled the rim and popped out. It bounced to Nick, who went up for an effortless jump shot that hummed through the net from fifteen feet.

"One down," said Nick. "Four to go."

"Three. The last man doesn't ever have to leave."

"Right. Three to go."

SEVENTEEN

On the next Monday, Mr. Rockwood told Albert he wanted to see him in his office after lunch. Albert tried to read his face, but there was nothing there—just the Rockwood mask.

Albert skipped lunch; nothing looked good. He sat for a time at a table with Nick and Princess and Small Dog, and watched them eat. Except Small Dog, who wasn't eating either. Albert figured he had other things on his mind. Like a four-thousand-dollar baseball card.

When the butterflies got to be too much, Albert walked outside and headed for the gym. He glanced at the football field, where two older guys were playing catch. Beyond them, the field met the far straightaway of the running track, and a lone figure stood, as still as a small tree, staring down the track.

Albert stopped and watched, and as he did the figure crouched low and took off, sprinting into a strong headwind. He looked tight but disjointed at the same time, struggling down the track, planting one foot in front of the other. He slowed, cutting his stride to baby steps, and launched himself from the ground. Until that moment, Albert didn't realize who the kid was. Yuno. No one else ran like that, or jumped like that. It was a pitiful jump. Yuno barely cleared the ground, landing maybe a body-length—a short body-length—from where he'd taken off. Albert felt a twinge of some kind of feeling for Yuno and started toward him. But the two big kids had quit throwing the football and were walking toward Yuno, too. Albert decided to stay out of their way. Yuno would have to figure out the long jump on his own.

Mr. Rockwood's office door was half-open, and Albert could see him at his desk, but he knocked anyway.

"Come in." Mr. Rockwood looked up as Albert walked into the small, cramped room. Boxes and assorted athletic gear lined the walls. Mr. Rockwood motioned to a folding chair next to his desk. "Sit down."

Albert sat, looking past Mr. Rockwood's head at a poster on the wall—a picture of a long jumper hitting the pit, sand kicking up around him. The strain of effort distorted his face, and Albert saw something else there, too—joy, maybe, or wonder. Big letters at the top of the poster said, WHERE DREAMS CAME TRUE. At the bottom were the words, 1968 OLYMPIC GAMES.

Mr. Rockwood turned in his chair, following Albert's gaze. "Bob Beamon," he said. "People said twenty-eight feet was impossible. He went more than twenty-nine—just skipped twenty-eight entirely. Then people said it was a fluke—some kind of accidental high-altitude mark that would never be beaten. Now it's been beaten." He pivoted back in his chair, facing Albert again. "So don't ever let anyone tell you that something is impossible, Mr. Alger, or even out of reach. You'll never know if you can attain a goal until you've given it your best effort. And if you give it your best effort and don't make it, you'll have nothing to be ashamed of."

Albert nodded, trying to look Mr. Rockwood in the eye, but he couldn't keep his eyes off the poster. What would it be like to fly like that, to make the sand explode, to stand in front of millions of people and have a medal hung around your neck?

"Study it, Mr. Alger. Think about the work, the years and years it took to get to that point." He reached for the phone. "Excuse me a minute," he said. He punched in the numbers. Albert's eyes wandered to a spot on the wall next to the poster, where a silver medal hung mounted in a frame. Something was written under the medal. Albert couldn't read it from this distance, but it had to be Mr. Rockwood's. Albert wondered how he could ever get one of his own. Would hard work be enough? If he couldn't be a long jumper, could he be the best at some other event?

"Mrs. Garza, please," Mr. Rockwood said into the phone. Mrs. Garza was the school librarian.

Mr. Rockwood swiveled his chair around, his back to Albert, who walked over to inspect the medal. The inscription read, SECOND PLACE, DECATHLON, BIG SKY CONFERENCE TRACK AND FIELD CHAMPIONSHIPS, 1968.

Albert shook his head and went back to his seat. A decathlete had to be good at ten different events. Albert was having a hard time learning the basics of one.

"Connie?" Mr. Rockwood said. "This is Sam. How are you?"

Sam? Albert hadn't pictured Mr. Rockwood's first name as Sam.

"You have it?" Mr. Rockwood said. "That's great. I was hoping to take it home tonight. I'll come by in a few—" He stopped, listening. "That would be nice of you," he said finally. He hung up, swiveled back toward his desk, and pressed his fingers into his forehead for a moment, closing his eyes as if he'd forgotten that Albert was still sitting there.

"I believe that we were discussing work," he said abruptly. "The reason I asked you here is to tell you that you've done a very good job with your tasks in the gym. Consequently, I'm releasing you from any further obligation. You no longer need to help out."

"But I still have a month left." Was Albert supposed to be happy?

"I realize that. But as I said, you've earned some

time off for good behavior. And I'm not going to be able to get to school as early from now on. At least, not for a while."

"I can work on my own. I know what to do now. I can have it all finished by the time you get here."

Mr. Rockwood looked at him for a long moment. "If you wish to continue the jumping, you may do so. And since you won't be doing the tasks, you'll have that much more time for training."

Albert had gotten himself in good enough shape that he could use more time now. He thought about the improvement he'd be able to make with a whole hour a day to work out. "Can I?" he said.

"You may, as long as you confine your activities to training. I just don't want to find all of the balls deflated." Mr. Rockwood smiled—a real, whole-face smile.

Deflated. As in tires. Albert got it. "I'll just run and jump and stuff."

"I'm sure you will. And if I arrive early enough, I'll take a look at your progress."

Albert heard a tap on the door, and turned to see Mrs. Garza hurry in with a book in her hand. "Here you go, Sam." She put it on his desk. "I hope it helps. I'm off to lunch."

"Thanks, Connie," Mr. Rockwood said to her back. The door closed and she was gone.

Albert glanced at the book: *The Trumpet of the Swan*. He'd read the story himself, several times, in fact. But why did Mr. Rockwood want a kids' book? Albert hadn't thought about him having kids.

"Which reminds me," Mr. Rockwood said. "I've got a book I was going to let you read on track and field, but I left it in my car. It's got a valuable section on long jumping. Come back here after your last class, and I'll have it for you."

"Thanks."

"You're free to go now, Mr. Alger."

"Okay." Albert got to his feet. "I'll be back after school."

"Good." But Mr. Rockwood wasn't looking at Albert. He'd picked up *The Trumpet of the Swan* and was staring at the cover. He had an expression that Albert hadn't seen on him before—distant and watery-eyed. Albert turned and headed for the door.

EIGHTEEN

A woman's voice said "Come in" when Albert knocked on the office door late in the afternoon. The other P.E. teacher sat at her desk, but Mr. Rockwood wasn't there. "Albert?" She looked up from a stack of papers.

"Yes."

"Mr. Rockwood had to leave, but he asked me to give this to you." She handed a big book to Albert. The other book—*The Trumpet of the Swan*—sat on the corner of Mr. Rockwood's desk.

"Is he coming back?" Albert asked.

"Not today. He had to take care of some unexpected business."

"Do you know if he left that on purpose?" Albert asked, pointing at the book.

"I don't. He left in a hurry. Why?"

"I heard him tell somebody—Mrs. Garza—that he wanted it for tonight."

"He must have forgotten it."

"Can I take it to him?"

"I don't see why not. Do you know where he lives?"

Definitely. Albert definitely knew where he lived. "I think I can find it."

"Go for it," she said.

Albert picked up the book. "Thanks," he said, and started for the door.

"Albert," she said, "I hear you're a long jumper."

A long jumper? Albert didn't think of himself as a long jumper—not yet, anyway. "I guess." He felt his face turning red.

"I could tell just by looking at you. Keep working at it."

"I will." This time he hurried out the door, hiding his face from her—and his grin. She'd called him a long jumper. He couldn't wait to get to the gym tomorrow.

Mr. Rockwood's driveway was empty when Albert made his first pass. He took off for the shopping center, for the bookstore. He'd give Mr. Rockwood some time to get home.

Forty-five minutes later, it was almost dark. If Mr. Rockwood wasn't home by now, Albert would just have to forget it.

But he was home. Lights shone from the windows as Albert pulled up in front.

Albert approached the door. He heard voices drifting from the open window. Maybe Mr. Rockwood wouldn't appreciate an unexpected visitor. Albert detoured to the window, ducking down as he got closer. The drapes were open, and light poured out onto the lawn.

He crouched under the window, his mouth dry. He needed either to give Mr. Rockwood the book or get out of there. Maybe if he could just take a quick look, he'd know if Mr. Rockwood had company.

He inched his head above the windowsill and peered inside. Across the living room, an old woman sat propped up in a chair. *And she was looking right at Albert.*

Run, he thought. Hide. But something stopped him. She *wasn't* looking at him. And she wasn't old. Not much older than Albert's mom. But her eyes were dark and sunken. Her thin, dull hair had been neatly brushed around the hollow cheeks, the milky, transparent skin of her face. Once, not long ago, she'd been beautiful.

Mr. Rockwood hurried into the room. He arranged a blanket gently around the woman's bony shoulders, angled a cap on her head, and kissed her on the cheek. Albert realized she was the same person he'd seen at the window that other night.

Mr. Rockwood sat in a chair next to her and opened up a small book. He began reading to her, a story Albert remembered from *The House at Pooh Corner*—the one about Tigger getting unbounced.

The woman's face brightened as Mr. Rockwood went on, nearly reciting the story from memory, doing a very authentic job with the voices. Albert recognized

Piglet's voice from his last visit to Mr. Rockwood's house.

Mr. Rockwood finished the story and stood up. He smiled at the woman. She smiled back, but her eyes didn't.

He set the book on a table and eased her from the chair. Arms locked around each other, they walked slowly from the room and out of sight.

Albert ducked down and hurried from the window. Now he knew what *The Trumpet of the Swan* was for, but it was too late for tonight. He'd give it to Mr. Rockwood first thing in the morning—just tell him that he rode by, but it looked like nobody was home. He couldn't tell him what he'd seen; he didn't even know what he'd seen. What was wrong with her? Something bad. Something really bad.

NINETEEN

You busy tonight, Mom?" Albert asked the next morning at the breakfast table.

She looked over at him, a gentle wariness in her eyes. "Not that I know of, honey. Why?"

"My books are all in storage, right? My old ones, I mean."

"Yes."

"Can you take me to the storage place tonight?"

"To get your books?"

"Just a few. Just a few old ones."

"How about right after dinner?" his mom asked. "If you can find a place for them."

"Oh, I'll find a place for them, Mom. I've already got one picked out."

That night he sorted through a big box of books. A long time ago, his mom had said he should save them. Someday he might want to read them to his kids. And he'd laughed at the idea.

But now he was glad he hadn't given them away. Turning their pages was like visiting old friends. Friends that he'd only remembered in his dreams.

Memories came drifting back of times when pictures told the story. When the words were just black trains rolling across the page that his dad or mom miraculously transformed into tales of frogs and princesses. And bears and little girls with golden hair. And a wicked witch in a candy house and the children she invited to dinner.

Albert picked out his favorites and stacked them on the desk. From the stack he chose his top three. Finally, he picked one of those—a gift from his aunt on the day he was born, a thick green book filled with fairy tales and illustrations from another time and place. Solemn princesses, icy queens, lumpy toads, bad-tempered trolls, and nightmarish creatures of the forest ghosted their way through the pages of the book.

He wrapped the book in brown paper, taped it up tightly, put it in his book bag, and looked at his clock. Ten-fifteen, it said. Why did he feel so awake? He needed to get to bed. He rummaged through his bag and pulled out his math book. If anything could put him to sleep in a hurry, this would do it. He crawled under his covers and opened the book. Five minutes later he drifted off.

Albert biked to school before the first light of morning. He talked the custodian into letting him in, but Mr. Rockwood's office was closed up and dark. Albert removed the package from his bag, wrote "Sam" on it with his best adult handwriting, and tried sliding it under the door. Too fat. He found the wall compartment marked ROCKWOOD. The book fit— barely. Not the safest spot to leave it, but it would have to do.

He shuffled into the gym. But for once he didn't feel like being there. He felt tired from staying up late and getting up early after a restless night. He was determined to get his routine in, but he didn't expect much out of it.

His warmups were tough; he had to drag his body through the exercises. But gradually he warmed up, and by the time he broke a sweat, he'd started getting some energy. Maybe this wouldn't be so bad, after all.

He waltzed through his first jump, slow and mechanical, saving his energy. But he looked down at his mark on the mat and got a surprise: he'd hit eight feet—just six inches short of his best effort so far. Suddenly a little knot of excitement began tightening up his insides. But now his body felt loose, and he bounced off the mat and jogged back to his starting spot. Maybe this would be a special day.

For a long moment, he toed the mark, arms pumping, crouching, eyeing the free-throw line. Then he took a deep breath and tore away, gaining speed as he approached the line. At the last instant he looked up, staring at the basket, and jumped. Stay loose, he told himself. Ride the air. Reach for the rim.

He landed and rolled forward, ending up on his

hands and knees. Before his mark had a chance to disappear, he turned around and found it. At first he couldn't believe it. He stared, wondering if maybe the old chalk line had been moved.

He chalked the new mark and ran to the equipment room for the tape measure. When he stretched it out from the free-throw line, it went to nine feet, four inches—ten inches past the old mark. He crouched and jumped, letting out a loud yell, his fist in the air. He wasn't tired anymore. Nine feet, four inches would get him over the river. Not by much, but it would get him safely to paydirt.

The rest of the time he spent trying to beat his new mark. Even though every jump came close—he felt as if he were in a groove now—he couldn't improve on it. But he still had weeks—he hoped—to get better.

An hour after Albert got home from school that afternoon, Nick called.

"Alibi." Just the name and then nothing else.

"Something on your so-called mind, Sponge Brain?"

"Willie Mays, Alibi," Nick said finally. "Willie's on my mind. I just found out that my folks are thinking about having a house built." He let the news sink in for a moment. "Think how long that'll take."

"Months." Albert couldn't believe it.

"Lots of months!" Nick shouted.

Or years. Albert had seen Nick's dad take a half-hour to decide what tie to wear. What were the odds of the same guy making quick decisions on something as major as building a house? There were only four of them left now; Albert should have had a better chance. Instead, he felt as if he had no chance. He didn't know what to say. Congratulations? He didn't think so.

"Hey, Alibi. I only said they were *thinking* about building their own house. They think about a lot of things."

"Sure." Albert hung up the phone and stepped outside for the newspaper. There had to be something in the paper to get his mind onto other things. He only got as far as the front page before he saw it.

There was a large photo near the bottom of the page. In it, a man and woman sat on a couch, close together, his arm around her shoulders. The man—Mr. Rockwood—was trying to smile but not making a very good go of it. The woman had a scarf on her head now instead of a baseball cap. Over the picture and the accompanying story ran the headline, "Couple Battles Insurer over Benefits."

Albert perched on the edge of the living room chair and read. The article contained some new words, like *impairments, exclusions, contractual provisions, disallowed procedures,* but Albert got the gist of it: Mrs. Rockwood—she was Mrs. Rockwood—had had surgery and chemotherapy for breast cancer. When the cancer came back, she'd had more chemotherapy. It didn't work, and now her doctors wanted to do a bone marrow transplant. But the insurance company wouldn't approve the procedure; they said it was experimental and expensive. So now Mr. and Mrs. Rockwood were fighting the decision. Mr. Rockwood had hired a lawyer and gone to the insurance commissioner, but they'd already spent their life savings on the medical bills they'd piled up so far.

It looked as if they'd hit a dead end, and time wasn't on their side. Mr. Rockwood figured that the insurance company would just drag its feet until it was too late for any kind of treatment to have a chance. And it wouldn't have to stall for long; she needed the transplant now. So he was going to take her to New York, where he'd heard of a doctor who'd successfully treated cancer patients using alternative methods, at a fraction of the cost of conventional care. Mr. Rockwood said they'd raise the money somehow— borrow it if they had to—and head to New York as soon as they could make arrangements.

An idea jumped into Albert's thoughts, big and bold and demanding; he tried to pretend it wasn't there. But it wouldn't go away—the idea that a car wasn't the best use of the last-man money, that if he should somehow get the money, he could give it to Mr. Rockwood.

Albert conjured up an image of his dream car, winding its way up a mountain highway. The picture faded until the highway was empty except for a lone bicycle creeping up the shoulder, powered by the muscular legs of an older, more mature version of himself.

He gave in. He knew it was right, and he wasn't going to fight it.

He returned to the article. The name of the reporter caught his eye this time: Maggie Heller. Special to the

Herald. He knew the name. He ought to. She'd changed his life—a lot of lives—in the past few months. But he didn't know she wrote for newspapers. Albert had been there when she'd met Mr. Rockwood; maybe he'd told her his story that day.

Albert took one last look at the picture. He'd seen enough to know that now he really *had* to be the last man. But Yuno, Princess, and Nick still stood in his way.

What if he told Nick and the other guys about Mr. and Mrs. Rockwood? Would they be willing to disband the club, sell the card, and turn over the money to Albert? Maybe, but they'd all have to agree to the plan. Nick would have to go along with it. Albert remembered how Nick's eyes came to life when he first saw the card, how he fought against the idea of selling it, and how he thought Mr. Rockwood was a creep. Would he be willing to give up the card now for Mr. Rockwood's wife? The idea floated into Albert's mind like an overinflated balloon, bobbed there for an instant, and exploded. Nick would protect that card until he was old and wrinkled and Rockwood was a name on a weathered stone in some graveyard.

For a moment Albert wondered what would happen if Princess or Yuno won. But it was a short moment, and he didn't like the answer: their chances of winning were no better than his, and what if he couldn't convince them to give it to Mrs. Rockwood?

No one else in the club knew the real Mr. Rockwood, and Mrs. Rockwood was a complete stranger. So it would have to be up to Albert, and it would have to be soon. In the meantime, he couldn't do anything but wait, and hope for some kind of miracle.

What remained of the club made it through the rest of the week intact. Despite his continuing pessimism, Albert still couldn't help but think about being the last man. After all, his mom and dad weren't exactly breaking their backs to find a house. And there wasn't any harm in dreaming, was there?

It was the following Monday when the next member announced his exit.

The phone rang, startling Albert from an afternoon snooze. His track and field book flew from his lap and landed on the floor. "Princess is history," Nick's voice said when Albert got the phone to his ear. "Three left, Alibi."

Albert sat back down. "Princess? He's moving?"

"I just saw him outside. He said to tell you and Yuno."

"Was he upset?"

"As upset as he ever gets. I think he said 'bloody house'."

"Sounds like him," Albert said. "Three left, huh?" It wasn't really sinking in yet.

"Temporarily."

"You must be getting excited. Two more and you've got it."

"Yeah, I think you should just give it up, Alibi. My folks haven't even talked about a house lately."

"When chickens grow lips, Sponge Brain. Or when my folks put their names on a dotted line. That's when I'll concede."

"Whatever," Nick said, and hung up.

TWENTY-ONE

n the third Saturday of October, it happened: Albert's parents found a house.

"You'll like it," his dad said.

Albert looked up from his book at their grinning
faces. How could they be happy at a time like this?

"It's supposed to be open at one o'clock, according
to the sign," his mom said. They stood at the door,
coats on, ready to go.

"Come see it with us," his dad said.

Albert shrugged his shoulders. What difference did
it make, anyway? Nick was going to be here until someone built a house on the moon. "Okay."

They drove away from the apartments and out of
the neighborhood. Albert kept glancing at his watch.
Five minutes since they'd left home. Then ten. A long
bike ride from familiar surroundings, and they were
still going. "Couldn't you find anything farther away?"
he asked. But did it matter? Who knew where the other
guys would be moving?

At last they left the highway and turned into a
housing development. SHY ANN WOODS, the sign at
the entrance said. And in smaller letters, HORSE ACRE
HOME SITES. A small sign slapped diagonally across

the big one said, GOING FAST.

Albert wondered what a horse acre was. It sounded like Small Dog's kind of place. Albert pictured old Small Dog out in his big backyard, cooking beans and spitting, his horse tethered to a tree. Mournful country music muffled the sounds of nearby grazing cattle.

They followed the winding road past shiny new homes on big lots. The only houses that didn't look occupied had SOLD signs stuck in the front lawns. They really were going fast. But not fast enough.

A sudden thought hit Albert between the eyes. "How'd you find out about this house?" he asked.

"Why?" his dad said.

"I mean, did a real estate guy tell you about it?"

"No," his dad said. "We were just out exploring."

"Some friends at work told me this was a nice area," his mom said.

It *was* a nice area, Albert decided as he looked out the back window. Maybe it wouldn't be so bad living here. But what about the money for Mrs. Rockwood?

They turned left, into a cul-de-sac.

"That's it straight ahead." His dad pointed to a gray house at the end of the short street. A woman was out in front attaching something to the FOR SALE sign.

"Oh, no," his mom said.

They pulled into the driveway, and Albert could see that the woman was stapling a SOLD sign to the realty sign. Oh, no, Albert thought, smiling to himself.

His mom rolled down her window. "When did it sell?" she asked the woman.

"Just this morning."

His mom slumped down in her seat. His dad looked at her and patted her on the hand. Albert couldn't help but feel sorry for her. A little sorry, anyway. "There'll be plenty of other houses, Mom," he volunteered. He hadn't seen her this disappointed in a long while.

"Uh-huh," she muttered. And then to the real estate woman: "May we look inside anyway? I'd like to see it again."

"Sure," the woman said. "And I can take your names in case this deal doesn't go through."

They walked through the house with the woman on their heels. It was nice. It smelled new. And she pointed out all of its "features." Like a giant whirlpool bathtub in the master bathroom. And French doors opening onto a big deck in the backyard. Albert didn't notice any horses tied to a tree, though.

"May I get your names on an offer?" she asked Albert's parents on the way out.

His dad looked at his mom, who nodded and said, "I like it. It's very nice."

"And unfortunately it was the last one left in the development," the woman said. "But you never know what might happen."

Albert hoped that *nothing* would happen.

The next day the apartment's swimming pool was closing down. Winter weather had set in, gray and drizzly and cold. Early in the afternoon, Albert called Nick. They met at the pool and jumped into the steaming water just as their skin was turning into twin maps of strange, pink, goose-bumped planets.

The pool felt warm, and they lazily trod water. Chin deep, Albert let the heat sink in, relaxing him all the way to his bones. The only thing he heard was Nick, gulping mouthfuls of water and spouting them skyward like a fountain.

"You know where that water's been?" Albert asked.

"No, Alibi. Where?!" Nick screamed suddenly, grasping his throat and thrashing around. His convulsions abruptly stopped. Eyes closed, he slipped beneath the surface of the pool.

Albert just kept floating. He'd seen this act. After holding his breath as long as he could, Nick would torpedo his way to the top, spouting another gusher and laughing. Albert turned his back and paddled toward the shallow end of the pool.

Seconds passed. He closed his eyes and waited for the eruption of water. Nick was doing a good job this time. He'd stayed under longer than usual.

The gate latch clicked and he heard Yuno's voice. "I've been looking for you, Alibi."

"Why—" Albert began, but Yuno was staring down into the pool, frozen in his tracks. His mouth worked open and closed, but no sound emerged.

Finally, the gears in his voice box meshed with those in his brain. "Hey," he said. "Hey!" he shouted, pointing down into the pool. "Hey! Hey! Hey! Hey!"

Nick's act had found a believer. Albert decided he'd better tell Yuno what was going on.

It was too late. Yuno took two steps and launched himself into the air, arcing out over the pool. He was going to the rescue, clothes and all. He went under just as Nick broke the surface, rocketing skyward, looking puzzled.

"Your rescuer," Albert said.

Yuno popped up, saw Nick grinning at him, and climbed disgustedly from the pool. He stood on the edge, dripping, glaring at Nick. "Funny. Very funny."

"I was just fooling around with Alibi, Yuno. I didn't even know you were around. What are you doing here, anyway?"

Yuno turned to Albert, his jaw set. "I came to talk to Alibi," Yuno said, ignoring the puddle that was forming around his shoes.

"About what?" Albert asked. He climbed out of the pool; Nick followed him.

"Your parents put their names on a waiting list for a house in Shy Ann Woods yesterday," Yuno said. "My parents, you know, bought it."

Albert heard what he was saying, but it didn't sink in at first.

"My parents are the reason your parents didn't buy it," Yuno said.

"That was lucky," Albert said. "For me, that is."

"That's what I was thinking," Yuno said.

"So you came here to tell me that?" Albert asked.

"Yeah," Yuno said. "And I was thinking that if you end up as the last man, you should, you know, split the money with me."

Albert smiled. "You're kidding, right?"

"No," Yuno said. "You wouldn't have a chance if it weren't for my parents."

"Your brain's been affected by the cold." Albert had heard of hypothermia doing stuff like that.

"I expect you to, you know, split it with me," Yuno said.

Albert didn't feel like humoring him. "Sure, Yuno," he said. "You just wait by your new mailbox for the money to, you know, arrive." He patted Yuno on his wet head, picked up his towel and shirt, and walked away.

"Thanks for saving my life, Yuno." Nick tossed his towel to Yuno. "You can give me this later."

And they were down to two.

TWENTY-TWO

For the next week, Albert cringed every time his mom or dad said his name; he was sure they were about to spring the bad news on him—the ultimate bad news. Maybe he shouldn't care; Nick seemed to have the contest locked up. But Albert kept remembering Bob Beamon and his magical jump. No one had thought he'd ever get to twenty-nine feet, but he hadn't given up on his dream. Why should Albert?

Somehow he made it to Saturday morning, but then he had a big problem: he'd run out of things to keep his parents' minds occupied. He'd talked his dad into a trip to the car wash, but that was it. And with nothing planned for the rest of the weekend, his parents would be free to do as much house hunting as they wanted. All he could think about was moving, and the baseball card, and Mrs. Rockwood. And the fact that Mr. Rockwood had been at school every day, which meant he hadn't taken her to New York or any-place else, which meant no big money had come rolling in.

Even his long jumping had suffered during the week. He hadn't gotten any worse, but he hadn't improved, either. And he considered that a step backward. Maybe the pressure was getting to him.

The trip home from the car wash took three minutes. He walked in the door and saw the newspaper opened on the coffee table—to the real estate section.

"It's for you, Albie," his mom said, holding up the phone.

"Alibi?" Nick's voice sounded different—cheerful, but forced.

"Sponge Brain."

"How ya doin' today?"

Albert wondered what Nick was going to try to sell him. "Pretty good," he said. "So far."

"I need to ask you something."

"Go ahead." Albert could feel his defensive armor clanking into place.

"Well," Nick began. Did Albert hear a small tremor in his voice now? "You know how my dad's a big baseball card fan?"

Albert knew about Nick's dad. His card collection was probably ten times as big as Nick's. But what did that have to do with anything? "Yeah . . ." he said.

"If you end up being the last man, would you be willing to sell the card to him? Fair market value, of course. And he'd give you cash." His voice wavered and cracked as he rushed the words out.

"What difference does it make, Sponge?" Albert asked. "You're the sure bet to win. He should be asking you. And what did you tell him for, anyway?"

"Would you sell it to him?" Nick asked again, his voice rising.

Albert thought a moment. He might as well humor Nick. "Four thousand? Would he give me four thousand for it?"

"The book says thirty-eight hundred."

"It's worth four, Sponge. You said so yourself."

"He'd give you four."

"I'd take it, then. If he'd give me four, I'd take it. If I end up the last man."

"You are." Nick's voice was a bare whisper.

"What?" There had to be some catch.

"You're the last man, Alibi. My folks bought a house Wednesday, and the builder's gonna let us rent until the paperwork's final. We're moving Monday."

"Monday?" Albert felt as if someone had vacuumed out the inside of his skull.

"Yeah. Even Yuno's gonna outlast me. He's not leaving till Tuesday."

"What happened?" Albert asked. "I thought your parents wanted to build a house."

"I told you they were just thinking about it. They changed their minds, even though I gave them every reason I could think of why they shouldn't."

"Including the last man's club?"

"Only as a last resort. I think my dad was actually

tempted, but he didn't think it would be fair. Neither did my mom. And she loves the house they found."

"I'm glad."

"But my dad did say he'd buy the card. An investment, he told my mom."

"And what's in it for you?"

Nick didn't answer for a long moment; Albert pictured a half-guilty grin spreading across his friend's face. "My dad said it'll be mine someday," Nick said finally. "All I need to do is make it through college."

It was Albert's turn to smile. Nick's dad had made a good bargain. Either he'd keep the card, or his son would make it through college. And if anything could make Nick want to do well in school and graduate from college, that card was it.

"So you didn't lose after all," Albert said.

"I guess not. But I'm gonna have a long wait."

"When will he give me the money?"

"As soon as he sees the card."

"Today?"

"You're going up there today?"

"Why not?"

"By yourself?"

"Unless you want to come."

"I can't. I have to go see the house with my parents and then go to Seattle. We won't be back till late. My dad would take us up tomorrow, though."

The thought of getting a ride to the trail was tempting, but Albert didn't want to wait—not even one day. He needed the money. "I'll go today," he said. "By myself."

"Why?"

Albert thought about explaining, but Nick wouldn't understand. "I want to. It's what I want to do."

"What about the river? How you gonna get across it? We moved the timber away, remember?"

"I've been working on jumping. Mr. Rockwood helped me out. I'm pretty good at it now."

"Good enough?"

"Yeah. I think."

"Take Yuno with you. He can help you with the timber. You can walk across."

"I don't need the timber," Albert said, trying to sound convincing. "And Yuno's mad at me, anyway. He wouldn't go."

"So you're really going by yourself?"

"Tell your dad I'd like the money by tomorrow morning. Can he get it today?"

"I guess so. I think the bank's open today."

"So I'll see you in the morning?"

"Yeah," Nick said. "Hey, Alibi . . ."

"What?"

"Be careful, okay? And if you decide not to try it, we'll go tomorrow."

"Okay. Hey, Sponge."

"Yeah?"

"Who was your real estate person?"

Silence. Then a sigh, long and drawn out. "I don't want to talk about it."

"See you." Albert wondered if Nick had ever heard about playing with fire. He hung up and walked back to the living room, his insides rumbling. He'd gotten what he'd been hoping for. Why didn't he feel better about it?

"Want to go for a ride, Albie?" his mom asked. "We thought we'd look at some houses, have lunch, and maybe take in a movie."

Albert was tempted. His parents' plans sounded a lot better—a lot safer—than what he saw for himself the rest of the day.

"I told some of the guys I'd go bike riding with them," he said.

"Where?" his dad asked.

"Uh, up toward the river, I think." Why did they need to get curious now?

"Not swimming this time of year," his mom said.

"No, Mom, just a ride—the last one this year, probably."

"You need to be careful on that highway, now," his dad said. "It might be slick."

"And make sure you're off it before it starts getting

dark," his mom said. "Those logging trucks won't see you."

Albert remembered the truck that had blown by him on a day not so long ago—a day that seemed a lifetime away. For a moment he could smell the exhaust and feel the hot cushion of air as if the truck had just plowed through the room. "Don't worry," Albert said. "I won't bike that road at night."

Ten minutes later, he'd packed a sweatshirt and flashlight in his backpack and put on his best jumping clothes—a T-shirt and shorts and his newest low-tops. On the way out the door, he added his Husky cap for good luck. He might need it. Deep down, in the chilly, trembling part of his soul, he thought he might need it.

TWENTY-THREE

A lbert stopped below the entrance to the mine and looked at his watch: one-thirty. He'd made good time. And he felt good. His legs felt strong, his breathing came easy, even at this altitude.

The mountainside held still and quiet as he stared at the mine. He thought of the water—the dark river cutting through the floor of the mine—and a chill eased into his spine, freezing him to the spot. But a bird sang in a nearby tree—a short, clear song of joy and freedom—and the doubts shrank.

He took out his flashlight and scrambled up the rock slide. He clicked on the light and ducked in.

Albert heard the river, close by, strengthened by autumn runoff from somewhere up the mountain. He inched forward and shone his flashlight toward the wall where they'd left the timber. But something looked different. He moved closer, until he saw the timber—the tip of it, anyway—sticking out from under a big pile of gray rock. Part of the wall had broken loose, burying the beam under tons of debris. Albert wouldn't be using it for a bridge, even if he wanted to.

But what about the rest of the mine? What if it had caved in farther back? What if the wall had crumbled, burying the card so deep he'd never get it out? Nick's perfect hiding place wasn't looking so good anymore.

The earthquake had done this—the same one that had rattled Granite Falls and turned Albert's insides to pudding. It had reached up here and shaken the mountain's insides, too, knocking down a wall as if it were made of toy building blocks. And what else had it done?

Albert swept the flashlight from side to side in front of him and moved toward the river, feeling its chill. The rest of the mine looked okay, but he couldn't see around the bend.

He reached the river's edge and looked down. The thought of testing that dark water descended on him like a darker cloud, and he shuddered, pulling back. But he made himself step forward again, check the footing, look for the best takeoff spot, the best place to land.

Once he'd decided on where to jump, he marked it with a big rock and headed back toward the entrance. He paced off twenty steps—about fifty feet, he figured—and pivoted around, facing the darkness, the black gash in the floor somewhere in front of him. He pointed his flashlight, found his marker, and jogged toward it, testing his legs. He paced off the distance again and turned, eyeing the crevasse. What was his margin of error? A good jump would allow him maybe six inches on each side. Not much.

Sweat trickled from his armpits, chilling his skin, and he bounced in place, until he felt warmer, loose, more under control.

Albert crouched, pumping his arms, concentrating on the crack, on an imaginary basketball hoop suspended ten feet above its far edge. He breathed deeply once, twice, three times, and took off, accelerating toward his marker. Halfway there he was flying, a rocket zooming toward a black hole, and he knew he wouldn't turn back. He watched the marker dancing in the flashlight beam and thought *footwork, timing, height.* He had to hit it just right. He had to plant just right.

And he did. He hit his mark at full stride, his left foot biting the ground inches from the edge. He pushed off and flew through the cool curtain of air above the river. He angled his legs behind him—in slow motion, it seemed—and then tucked them up and out, trying to delay his landing.

Eyes wide, legs poised like springs, he hit, both feet landing flat and true. He let his weight carry his upper body ahead. He couldn't afford to fall back—not this time. He pitched forward, dropped the flashlight, and rolled onto his knees and hands and side before coming to rest on his back, staring straight up at the blackness.

Albert fumbled for the flashlight, pointed it at the rough ceiling, and felt an eruption building up inside of him. He let it go, and it poured out, shaking his sides as it came. It grew into a laugh that filled the mine, bounced off the walls and floors and ceiling, and drowned out the sound of the river. The laugh changed to a shout of triumph, and he sprang to his feet, jumping and dancing and weaving toward the back of the mine. He'd made it. He'd made it across.

His right foot hit a rock, and he stumbled forward. The rock shouldn't have been there. He lost his balance and put his arms out to break his fall, waiting for the rough surface to bite into his hands. He waited. The bite didn't come. Only thin air—and a sickening feeling in the core of his stomach. And then he was hands down, head down, falling.

Albert felt cold explode all around him, and suddenly everything was wet, and dark. No, not just dark—black. He'd fallen into a hole filled with water, and now he was going down.

Albert stuck his arms straight out and spread his legs, trying to slow his descent. His hands hit bottom, rough and rocky, and he struggled to right himself, to decide in the blackness which way was up. Lungs burning, he forced himself to relax, to get his feet beneath him. He felt a current—a tug against his crouched body—and he pushed off, propelling himself toward what he hoped was the surface. Fear rose with him.

His head broke the surface and he gulped air—sweet, cool, air. He spun around, trying to get his bearings, but it didn't help. He couldn't see the sides of the hole—or whatever it was he'd fallen into. The earthquake had done a good job of rearranging the mine.

He stroked—once, twice—and hit a wall. Black water moved toward the wall and beneath it, flowing toward some dark place. Albert pushed off to the opposite side. Ten feet, he figured. He pulled himself along the wall and pushed off again; maybe eight feet. An eight-by-ten-foot hole in the floor, and he was lucky enough to have fallen into it. But how could he get out?

Albert felt panic rising inside him again, and he took deep breaths, trying to think about something positive. But he couldn't. The third bad thing had happened. It had taken awhile—long enough for him to shove the killer log and the earthquake to the back of his mind. But the third bad thing had happened.

He decided to look for a ledge, or some handholds. He looked up, trying to figure how far he'd fallen from the floor of the mine. He could see the dimmest of light above the rim of the hole. Light from the entrance, he guessed, and he figured maybe eight feet to the surface. Probably this was some kind of underground backwater of the river. Not much current, but possibly deeper, and just as cold, just as dark.

He continued on around the pool. How long could he stay up without at least something to hang onto? On his third circuit, he found a ledge protruding from the main wall a foot above the surface of the water. He measured it end-to-end: three feet long, maybe. He pulled himself high enough out of the water to gauge its width: a foot or so before it met the wall. Big enough to sit on, if he could get himself up. He held on one-handed and let his legs rest. He felt cold. His body wasn't getting used to this water.

He wondered if he could launch himself high enough from the ledge to grab onto the edge of the hole. Maybe it wasn't really eight feet to the floor. Maybe he wouldn't even have to jump.

First he had to get on the ledge. He discovered an underwater indentation in the rock at about the level of his knees, big enough to wedge his shoe into. Shoe stuck firmly in the wall, he push-pulled up from the water. He got a knee on the ledge and felt the rock bite into his skin. He pictured blood flowing from the wound, dripping to the water below, attracting some giant, subterranean, man-eating creature. He lifted the other knee up and shifted his weight, landing on his rear with his back to the wall.

Now he needed to stand up. He swung his feet onto the ledge and, using the wall for balance, slowly and carefully stood. He leaned against the rock, catching his breath, afraid to move.

He peered up at the opposite wall. He could make out its top edge, outlined against the glimmer of daylight. But it still looked like a long way up, maybe ten feet from the water to the floor of the mine. And if the outcropping was a foot above the water, more than two feet of wall still stretched above his tallest reach. He would have to jump that distance straight up off a slippery slice of rock, grab onto the floor—probably with one hand—and pull himself up. He'd gotten himself in good shape, but he didn't have a two-and-a-half-foot vertical leap. But what else could he do? How long would it be before someone figured out where he was? He couldn't wait that long.

He raised his right hand, bumping it along the lumpy surface until it was straight overhead. All he felt was wall—no ledge, no floor. He wanted to know how far it was, how far he had to jump, but he supposed it didn't matter. He needed to jump as far as he could. If that was enough, he had a chance to grab on. If it wasn't, he'd probably be back in the water.

Albert fought off a spasm of shivers, took a deep breath, and thought of the cold water inches below him. No, he told himself, and took two more breaths, thinking tall, high, slam dunk, Rocket Man. He needed to fly.

He jumped, twisting toward the wall. At the top of his jump he grabbed but came up empty. His hand scraped along the rock as he fell back, bracing himself for the water.

His left shoe brushed the edge of the ledge just before the cold hit him and he went under, feet first this time and not as deep. This time he knew where he was. He popped to the surface and looked up, getting his bearings, trying not to think about the trouble he was in. He paddled to the outcropping and grabbed on, getting his strength back.

After a few minutes he struggled onto the rock and got to his feet. But it was harder this time, and when he jumped, he didn't jump as high. He splashed into the water and swam back to the little shelf, feeling numb all over.

Albert waited on the outcropping this time, hoping some of the chill would leave him. But it didn't go away—even with a long routine of deep knee bends, even with a serious pep talk—and when he leaped, he came up short once more. He scraped his cheek and shoulder on the wall and landed on the shelf, struggling to keep his balance before he fell back in.

He swam to the ledge and hung on; this time he

wouldn't jump again. It might be the last time he could climb out of the water. He waited until the pain in his face and shoulder faded before boosting himself onto the outcropping and getting to his feet. But everything seemed harder; he felt stiff, and sore, and chilled to the bone. He'd run out of ways to help himself.

For the first time, Albert thought about dying in that hole. He tried to push the idea aside, but suddenly his mind filled with images of the people he'd leave behind if he didn't make it. He couldn't bear the thought of his mom and dad, of how his dying would affect them. He knew he had to fight. He knew somebody would come. He just had to be here when they showed up.

He felt as if he'd lost a lot of body heat already; he couldn't stop shivering, and his wet clothes just made him colder. Carefully he stripped off his shirt, wrung it out, and hung it on an inch-long knob of rock sticking out from the wall. It probably wouldn't dry, but at least he felt a little warmer without the wet cloth clinging to his skin.

He wondered what time it was. His watch still hung on his wrist, but he couldn't see it. He remembered arriving at the entrance at one-thirty. How long had he been in the mine? An hour? Two? He tried breaking down each little thing he'd done by how many minutes it might have taken, but he had a hard time with the addition. The cold must have gotten to him. Finally, he came up with one hundred eight minutes—close to two hours. Probably an exaggeration, but at least it gave him an idea.

So it wouldn't be dark for about three hours, which was when his parents would start wondering about him. But they had no idea where he was; they'd never find him on their own—not in time, anyway. They'd call his friends, but Small Dog, Princess, and Yuno wouldn't know where he was, either. And Nick, the only one who did know, wouldn't be home. His parents would call the sheriff, but the sheriff wouldn't be able to help—not soon enough. Then maybe—just maybe—they'd keep calling Nick until he got home late that night. If they did, he'd tell them where to look. If they didn't, he'd probably call sometime the next morning asking for Albert, and if Albert's parents were home, Nick would tell them then.

At best, if his mom and dad reached Nick that night, Albert figured he had another eight or nine hours to wait. If they didn't talk to Nick until the next day, he'd have to go twenty or more. Eight or nine seemed like a lifetime, but at least something he could maybe do. Why hadn't he just waited another day to come up? What difference would another day have made? But it was too late. He was here now, and he had to deal with it.

He couldn't imagine being much colder. He touched his shirt, but it felt as wet as ever. He never thought dry clothes would sound so good. But at least drinking water wasn't a problem. A whole reservoir of it was flowing by right below him.

He squatted down and reached into the water with one cupped hand. When he brought the hand to his lips, he felt it shaking with cold, and he wondered how much water had simply vibrated out. But some remained, and it tasted like no water he'd had before—cold and fresh and pure. He went back for more, again and again, until his thirst was gone. If only he could take care of his other problems that easily.

Time passed, and Albert grew colder. Worse, he was getting tired. No, not just tired—sleepy—and he knew what that meant. He'd read articles about hypothermia, and he recognized his sleepiness as a symptom. He got more water, drank it, splashed it on his face, and ran it down the back of his neck. But he could hardly feel it on his skin. He did some clumsy knee bends and toe raises, but they didn't help. And he was afraid to do anything more ambitious; if he fell off the rock now, he wasn't sure he could get back on.

After a while—a long while—the light overhead seemed to fade, but by then he wasn't sure. His eyes didn't feel right, and his head ached, and he just wanted to lie down somewhere and go to sleep. He touched his shirt again: still cold, but maybe not quite as wet. He put it on, struggling to get it over his head without losing his balance; his arms had stiffened and wouldn't do what he wanted. The shirt didn't make him any warmer, but he'd leave it on anyway. It would be too hard to get back off.

Albert leaned against the wall, feeling himself fading, and knew he needed to sit down or he'd fall. He lowered himself to a crouch, and finally a sitting position, knees tucked under his chin, left shoulder to the wall.

When he looked up again, he couldn't be sure he saw any light at all. After six o'clock, he thought vaguely; he might have only five or six more hours to wait. The thought made him fight down a knot of panic in his chest. He didn't know if he could last that long.

Maybe if he just got a little rest he'd feel better. If he could fall asleep, some time would pass. Somewhere in a deep, covered-up compartment of his mind, a voice was telling him that he might not wake up again. But a little sleep couldn't hurt. He'd just lean up against the wall so he wouldn't slip into the water, and catch a nap. He pressed his shaking shoulder against the rock. It would be easy to fall asleep now; the mine had gone completely black. He closed his eyes.

TWENTY-FOUR

The cemetery gate creaks as Albert closes it behind him and watches the sun slip behind the trees. Darkness is coming, and he doesn't want to be here after dark. He'll have to hurry. He runs up the hill past the tall gravestones of the wealthy and hurries to where the graves are marked by flat, metal rectangles buried in the ground. At last he spots it, off by itself on a little rise: a smooth headstone. He can read her name on it plainly. And he sees Mr. Rockwood's last wish for her: "Happily Ever After."

Tears are filling his eyes now, and the sky is growing darker. He kneels and leaves his presents: a tattered copy of Great Expectations *and a small red rose in a child's blue-and-white teapot. He stands quickly and turns to go; he wants to beat darkness to the gate. But his feet don't move, and then they begin to tremble. The ground shakes beneath him, side to side and up and down, and rolls like the wake from an ocean liner. He stumbles, tripping back down the little knoll, finally lurching to a stop on a grave marker. But a chill—a freezing cold—shoots up into his feet. When he looks at the stone, the words flash up at him in green neon lettering beneath a carving of a rattlesnake. "Don't Tread on Me," they say. The rattlesnake moves, its tongue flicking* out, searching, and Albert backs away, watching it slide off the marker. The ground lifts and drops, lifts and drops, and Albert staggers back, trying to get to the gate. Dusk has come, and the gate stands somewhere in the murk, beyond the shadowy tombstones and quaking earth.

A figure dressed in a baggy baseball uniform steps out from behind a swaying tree. His face is familiar—young and dark and friendly. "Gimme your fastball, kid," he says, smiling and lifting a bat from his shoulder, cocking it behind his head. "Your best one." He takes a step back, ready for the pitch, but the ground opens up beneath him and he plunges in. Albert hurries toward him, struggling against the heaving ground, but by the time he arrives the hole seals up and vanishes. In the distance the gate rises into view and Albert stumbles toward it, weaving around grave markers.

Without warning the ground cracks open and collapses. He steps off into space and falls, head first, down and down, before plunging into icy water. He fights to the surface, gasping for air, looking for a way out, but darkness surrounds him. Terrified, alone, he waits for the hole to close back up.

From somewhere in the distance, a voice calls. He listens, and it calls again, closer this time. His name. The voice is calling his name.

TWENTY-FIVE

He'd fallen in. Albert had gone to sleep and toppled into the water, and now he was trying to wake up, to stay up, to make his arms and legs move, to breathe, to find that outcropping of rock. The dream—the nightmare—was gone, and he was back to his real nightmare.

He followed the wall, fuzzy and shapeless against his numb, trembling fingers, until he found the outcropping. He held on with both hands, catching his breath.

He heard the voice again, the voice of his dream. Still far away, but closer, and this time he wasn't dreaming. He prayed that he wasn't dreaming. He waited, afraid he'd imagined it, afraid his own frozen throat wouldn't be able to answer.

"Albert!" the voice called once more. It wasn't his dad's voice, or his mom's.

"Here!" he shouted, but even in his own ears the word sounded muffled, smothered by the walls and the ceiling high overhead. "I'm here!" he yelled so hard that his throat ached.

"Alibi?" the voice said.

"Yuno!" Albert shouted.

"Alibi!" Albert could see a flashlight beam scanning back and forth overhead.

"Here!" Albert called. "In the water! At the bottom of a hole! A cave-in!" He watched the beam of light settle on the rim of the hole and travel slowly to one end and back to the other. Yuno had to be on the other side of the river. He had no way to get across. What now?

"You're in water?" Yuno asked.

"Yes!"

"How deep?"

"Over my head."

"For how long?"

"What time is it?"

"Almost seven."

"Five or six hours, off and on." An eternity. How much longer could he last?

"You're, you know, freezing." It was a statement, not a question.

"Get help, Yuno. You need to get help."

"Hold on for a few minutes, Alibi. I'll be right back."

A few minutes? Who did Yuno think he was kidding? How long would it take him to get back down the trail in the dark, ride his bike however many miles to wherever he could find the nearest phone, call someone, wait for them to get to him, and then lead them back to the mine? An hour, maybe, at best. Not a few minutes. He wanted to yell at Yuno, tell him not to leave. But what good would that do? He'd have some company while he froze to death or drowned. He had to let Yuno go.

Albert moved a little ways down the outcropping, testing his hands and arms. They felt clumsy, not a part of him, but somehow they still worked. He lunged up and out of the water, his legs churning beneath him. He landed on one knee, smiling through his pain. Just knowing that Yuno had found him had charged him with some extra spirit.

He rested for a moment, thinking of Yuno heading back down the mountain. The shivering was getting worse; the cold had crept deeper inside him. Concentrating hard, he got both knees under him before struggling to a squatting position. Finally he stood, pressed against the wall.

Above him, a light flashed against the ceiling. Yuno? Why had he come back? A moment later, he heard the sound of something hitting the floor. A sharp thud, a bounce, a skid. "Yuno?" he said. No answer. "Yuno!" he shouted.

"Yeah!" Yuno yelled back.

"What are you doing? What was that noise?"

"I threw a tree limb across. I think we can use it to get you out."

Out? How? He'd have to crawl out of the hole to get the branch first, and by then he wouldn't need it. "How am I going to get the limb, Yuno?" he yelled. A shudder ran through him, threatening to peel him from the wall, and he had to grab the shirt-hanger knob to regain his balance.

"I'll, you know, reach it down to you."

"How?"

"I'll jump it."

Jump it? A mud puddle, maybe. But not the river, not the moat. "Don't do it, Yuno!" Albert shouted. "Go get help."

"You can't wait that long."

Albert didn't argue; Yuno was probably right.

"I'm coming," Yuno said. "I'll be there in a minute."

Albert glimpsed another flash of light overhead. "Don't do it!" he shouted again, but he got no answer. He couldn't believe Yuno was going to try it. What if he didn't make it? They'd both need rescuing; Yuno might be worse off than Albert was; he'd be down in the crevasse and would have the river's current to battle. Yuno could die trying. "Go get help, Yuno!" he shouted, but even as the words came out, another shudder wracked his body. Still no answer from Yuno, and for a moment Albert thought maybe he'd gone. But seconds later, a piercing yell echoed through the mine. Albert waited for the sound of a splash, but it didn't come. Instead, he heard a thump, the clatter of loose rock, and a shrill cry—a whoop of triumph.

"The eagle has landed!" Yuno screamed.

Albert watched the flashlight beam dance through the air above him and pictured Yuno celebrating his accomplishment. In a moment, the beam found Albert's face, stinging his eyes, and he turned away.

"Sorry, Alibi," Yuno said. "You don't, you know, look good."

"I don't feel good."

"We'll get you out of there."

"I can't believe you're here, Yuno," he said.

In answer, Yuno shone the light under his chin. His face glowed red and ghostlike, suspended in the empty darkness of the mine. "It's me," he said.

"The best you've ever looked."

"I wish I could say the same for you," Yuno said. He pointed the flashlight at Albert's feet. "You been standing on that little ledge the whole time?"

"When I wasn't swimming."

Yuno whistled. "Hold on," he said. Something—the tree limb—eased over the edge. Albert could see it silhouetted against the ceiling, bare branches standing out like ribs from a spine. "I'm giving you the thick end," Yuno said. "It's not, you know, exactly flat, but I smashed it down some. If you can get it to sit on the rock, then I can hold up this other end while you climb out."

Climb out? Albert wasn't sure if he had the strength. But he was going to try. "Okay," he said. He reached up to guide the end of the limb down. It brushed his forearm, and he grabbed on, steering it toward the wall and his feet.

"Okay," he said, as the butt of the limb touched his foot. The end was uneven where it had split from the tree, but Yuno had pounded it down pretty well. Albert was able to get it firmly planted on the ledge.

Yuno played the flashlight up and down the length of the limb, giving Albert a chance to see what he had to work with. He guessed that it had broken off some kind of fir tree; it was straight, with evenly spaced branches, none more than a foot apart, like a ladder. A spark of excitement sent a warm wave surging through Albert's bones.

"Can you tilt it a few inches out and still hold it steady?" Albert asked through chattering teeth. "It's too close to the wall to give me footholds."

"I think so," Yuno said, "but I'll have to put the flashlight down."

Albert watched the flashlight beam move to the ceiling. It was near-dark again in the hole. "How's that?" Yuno asked.

Albert felt the space between the limb and the wall.

"About right," he said. "You got both hands on the limb?"

"Both hands, both knees, both feet."

Albert pictured him wrapped around the top of the limb like a pretzel, with only his rear end on solid ground. "Careful," he said.

"I'm not falling in," Yuno said. "Don't worry."

"I'm coming up." Albert blew on his hands one at a time, trying to get some feeling into them, and grabbed on. Slowly he put his weight on the first limb. Hold, he thought. Don't break. Don't put me back in that water.

And it held. He lifted his left foot, feeling for the next branch, and found it. His hands held on, and he pulled himself up. His right foot found another branch, and then his left, and he raised himself higher.

"I can see you, Alibi!" Yuno said. "You're getting close."

Albert made it to another branch, and another, and the next time his hand reached up he felt Yuno's foot.

"All right!" Yuno shouted, but he didn't move. His foot stayed pressed to the wood as if it had been glued on.

Albert climbed higher until his head was level with the floor of the mine, until he felt Yuno grasp him under both arms.

"Now!" Yuno twisted back from the hole, pulling Albert with him.

Albert let go of the tree and shifted his weight toward Yuno. He rolled, feeling solid ground beneath him, and lay on his back, enjoying the pain of sharp rocks pushing against his wet shirt and skin. He was out of the hole. He wasn't going to die down there. "I'm alive!" he croaked. He felt tears in his eyes.

Yuno sat down next to him. "You made it," he said.

"Because of you. You jumped across the river. How did you do that?"

Yuno took off his sweatshirt. "Put this on."

Albert struggled out of his wet shirt and put on the dry one. It felt thick and heavy against his skin. "Thanks, Yuno," he said, waiting to feel some warmth. "How did you jump across the river?"

"The same way you did. I, you know, practiced a lot. And a couple of eighth-graders helped me. They said Mr. Rockwood taught them everything there is to know about long jumping."

Albert remembered the lunch recess when he'd seen Yuno at the school track, practicing his jumping. He'd come a long way since then—he'd come further than Albert had. "We could've worked out together."

"You probably had things on your mind."

"No excuse to be a jerk," Albert said.

But then he thought of Mrs. Rockwood. The card was still somewhere in the mine.

We have to get the card!" Albert staggered to his feet. His head hurt, and he felt numb and dizzy.

Yuno gave him a worried look.

"Mrs. Rockwood's sick," Albert said. "The card—the money—is for her."

Yuno stood up. "Mrs. Rockwood doesn't, you know, need the money anymore."

The words didn't register at first, and then Albert knew what Yuno meant. "She's dead?"

"No. She isn't dead. The insurance company decided to pay for her operation."

Albert hadn't read the paper today. "Why did they decide to pay?" he said.

"Don't know. Maybe they didn't like the publicity."

"Probably." It didn't really matter why. At least now she'd get whatever care she needed. But the Rockwoods would still need more money. They'd gone broke just paying for the treatment she'd already had.

Albert and Yuno headed for the back of the mine. Albert's legs felt as heavy as driftwood tree trunks; his wet pants clung to him like cold mud. He shuffled along, trying to get his muscles and joints to work.

They rounded the bend, and Albert's heart sank. The near wall had been transformed into another rock slide. As they skirted around the slide, he wondered how much more of the mine had come down. What was up ahead?

But beyond the mound of debris, the wall stood straight and intact. Yuno moved the beam carefully along the floor. Albert stared, looking for the marker rock, and suddenly it appeared from out of the gloom, just as he remembered it.

"Two paces farther," Yuno said, taking two long strides along the wall. He bent down and dug with his hands. Albert tried to help, but his fingers felt stiff, as if they were webbed together like frog toes. The small, angular stones poked into his skin and sent pain shooting up his arms. He sat and watched Yuno uncover the sweatshirt and pull it from the hole. "Put this on," Yuno said. It was grimy and wrinkled, but dry, and Albert was glad to have it. He pulled it on over the other one.

"Looks good," Yuno said, examining the box. "Let's get out of here."

They passed the hole and approached the river. "I can't jump it, Yuno," Albert said. He could maybe do three feet. He took two steps and made a trial jump. But he barely left the ground, and when he landed his knees buckled, nearly sending him sprawling.

"I know you can't," Yuno said. "I'm gonna have to go across and find something to use for a bridge for you. Hold this," he said, handing the box to Albert.

Yuno directed the flashlight beam ahead at the crevasse, sweeping it from side to side until he found his landing spot. He backed up, giving himself some room to run, and took off. Albert held his breath and watched the light race toward the river, bouncing through the darkness—up and down, up and down—with every step Yuno took. Then it was flying, a low-level shooting star, crossing the chasm. For a long moment, Albert didn't breathe. Then he heard a thud, and the light looped once before stopping on the floor. Yuno had made it.

A moment later the flashlight moved, rising off the ground. "Crash landing." Yuno pointed the flashlight at his face. Albert could see what looked like a streak of blood on his cheek. "You hang on here," Yuno said. "I'm gonna go look for a log. Be right back."

"Hurry, Yuno," Albert said. The cold was still eating at him. But at least he wasn't going to drown in that giant black puddle. Yuno—the guy he thought wasn't even talking to him anymore—had saved his life.

Albert had counted to 374 by "thousand-ands" when Yuno set the flashlight down near the entrance, propping it up so the beam projected across the floor. "You okay, Albert?" he called.

"Great. You?"

"Got me a big hunk of wood here. At the entrance, anyway. Twelve feet long, probably, and stout."

Yuno headed back toward the mouth of the mine. After a few minutes, Albert could hear the sound of something heavy being dragged.

"Can you catch the flashlight?" Yuno asked.

"Maybe. If you leave the light on." Albert set the box at his feet.

"At least break its fall."

Albert saw the flashlight coming, saw it floating through the air right to him, but he couldn't handle it. He moved his arms, but his reflexes were shot. The flashlight hit his hands—cold, stiff boards—and bounced to the floor. But it stayed on; it didn't break. He picked it up and pointed it across at Yuno.

"Nice catch," Yuno said. He picked up the small end of the log and worked it into the air until it pointed at the ceiling. The bigger end sat two feet from the edge.

"Give me a target to go for."

Albert used the beam to find a spot directly across from Yuno. "How's this?" he said, focusing the light on the target.

"Looks good," Yuno said. "Better step back."

Seconds later Albert heard a grunt and caught a glimpse of Yuno jumping to the side as the log came down. It hit, solid and true, and bounced once before settling into the dirt.

"How much log you got over there?" Yuno said.

"Three feet, at least. Plenty."

"Throw the flashlight back over. I'll do the light."

Albert moved toward the crevasse, testing his arm. He could move it, but it felt as if he'd been lying on it wrong and it had fallen asleep. "Here comes," he said. He threw the flashlight—too low, too strong—and Yuno had to dive to catch it.

"What a grab," Yuno said. "Eat your heart out, Willie."

"Now what?" Albert asked.

"The box. And try to, you know, get it up in the air."

Albert retrieved the box. Two-handed, he lofted it toward Yuno. The light clattered to the ground as Yuno prepared to field the box. An instant later, Albert heard the box hit the ground.

"It's okay," Yuno said, inspecting it with the flashlight. "No dents. Nothing."

"My turn," Albert said. "Any suggestions?"

"In your condition, you're gonna have to sit down and scoot across."

Albert knew Yuno was right. But the way his muscles were working, he wasn't sure he could even make it across on his rear end. And if he didn't, the river would make him pay. He straddled the log and worked his way forward until his legs were dangling in the air. He sensed the water moving down below him. He took a deep breath and scooted forward again and again, and then Yuno was reaching out, tugging him in. The river was behind him. He'd made it.

They hurried from the mine, Albert struggling to get his legs to work. Outside, he put on the dry sweatshirt from his backpack. Three layers now, but it didn't help. He saw Yuno shiver in his thin T-shirt. The mine had been as cold as the inside of an icebox; it seemed only a little warmer out here. "You want your sweatshirt back, Yuno?" he asked.

"You need it worse than I do," Yuno said. "Let's get moving. I'll warm up in no time. You, too."

But Albert didn't warm up. The cold—the strange, numbing, sick feeling—stayed with him through the valley and up to the trail. He followed Yuno down the mountain, past the trees and undergrowth, over the stream, winding through the dark forest.

They reached the bike-hiding spot. Albert stood on the trail, swaying, while Yuno retrieved the bikes from the bushes. He flashed the light in Albert's face. "Can you ride?"

"Maybe." Albert lifted his leg over the bar of his bike. The effort nauseated him.

Albert pointed the bike down the path and pushed

off. But he lost his balance and dumped himself on the ground. He lay there, dizzy and shaking.

Yuno helped him to his feet. "Get on," he said, patting the seat behind him. "You ride a bike about as good as my little brother. But we didn't bring any training wheels."

Albert held on while the bike bounced along the trail, flew down long stretches of highway, wound through gentle curves, kept rolling. They reached a hill too steep for Yuno to pedal. He got off the bike and pushed, with Albert shuffling along behind him in his wet shoes. He could barely feel his feet.

At the crest of the hill, they got back on and accelerated into the quiet night.

Up ahead, a pair of headlights came around a bend in the road, followed by another. They slowed, then jerked to a stop a hundred feet away. Before Yuno could brake the bike, the car doors flew open, and people were running across the road.

Albert saw his dad, then his mom, then Yuno's parents. He heard their voices, felt their hands on him. They asked questions, but he couldn't listen, couldn't answer. And then he was walking—floating—to the car, supported by hands and arms. Over his shoulder, he said something to Yuno—thanks, he hoped it came out—and then he was sitting in the back seat, and his dad was taking off his wet clothes and covering him with a blanket and a coat and another coat. His mom sat next to him—almost on top of him—and draped herself around him like a sweater. The doors slammed shut.

Albert felt warmth moving from the heater into the air, weighing on his eyelids, pushing them down. The last thing he remembered was his dad's face—scared—in the rearview mirror.

TWENTY-SEVEN

Except for some muffled sounds from the hall, the hospital room was quiet. Albert rolled over and stared past the empty bed next to him, at the trees and buildings outside his window. Dusk was settling on the city of Everett.

They'd brought him here—the closest hospital —last night. He remembered some of it: staggering into the emergency room propped up between his parents, sitting in a hot tub with water to his chin, drinking cup after cup of hot chocolate and weak tea, lying under layers of thick blankets, feeling the blessed warmth creep back into his body. In between were short blank spells, and afterward a long one—a long night of sleep interrupted by vigilant nurses and attacks of the chills and dark dreams of darker places and black, icy water. Later, there were brighter, full-color dreams—of jumping, of taking off from the ground in slow motion and floating and not having to come down, ever.

He remembered his parents' faces nearby every time he opened his eyes, until finally he awoke and daylight was filtering into the room through the blinds, and they were gone, and he was warm. *He was warm.*

His mom and dad came back, looking tired but happy, followed by a doctor, who talked about exposure and hypothermia, and told them that she wanted to keep Albert in the hospital another two days. Yuno, who had spent time in the waiting room the night before, showed up next. With a scratch on his cheek nearly as big as his smile, he carried the tackle box proudly into the room and set it on Albert's bed.

"The reward, Albert," Yuno said. "It's finally yours."

"How did you find me, Yuno?"

"My parents are out in the lobby. They, you know, asked the nurse."

"Last night. How did you find me last night?"

"I saw Nick before he left. He told me you'd gone to the mine. He looked worried. He got me worried. The more I thought about it, the more nervous I got. I thought I was being kind of, you know, stupid, but I decided to go up there anyway."

"I'm glad you did."

"I figured I'd just meet you on the way back. But I didn't, so I kept going."

"Our parents—how'd they know where we were?"

"They didn't. They were just relying on what you'd told your mom and dad—that you were heading up toward the river. All I told mine was that I was going for a bike ride. They only found us because we were, you know, already on the highway."

"I owe you big-time."

"Forget it."

"I won't, but I need to ask you another favor."

"Sure."

"Nick's dad's buying the card from me. He was supposed to get me four thousand dollars at the bank yesterday. I want to give it to Mr. Rockwood, but I know he won't take it from me."

Albert explained his plan to Yuno, who was excited about helping out. He left with the tackle box tucked snugly under his arm.

Nick and his dad came next. Nick brought Albert five new packs of baseball cards. He helped Albert look through the cards, sitting close enough on the bed that Albert noticed the unmistakable smell of licorice. He smiled to himself, but didn't say anything. He was just glad to have Nick nearby. Nick's dad said he would get the Willie Mays money to Yuno as soon as he and Nick got back to the apartments.

Before they left, Nick said something that gave Albert the chills all over again: "We got home late last night, Alibi. Almost midnight, I think. If your parents would've had to count on me to tell them where you were, we couldn't have gotten to the mine until one in the morning. I'm really glad you made it."

Another hour would have been pushing it. Six or

seven more? No way. Albert didn't want to think about it.

"Next time, don't go alone," Nick said.

"There won't be a next time." Albert would never go back.

"You won't just want to *read* about stuff like that," Nick said. "There'll be a next time." He smiled and gave Albert a light punch on the shoulder. "See you Tuesday," he said. "At home."

Princess and his parents arrived next, then Small Dog and his mom. Albert told the story so many times that he didn't think his voice would take one more telling. They all—kids and parents—sat and listened each time, while Albert told of adventure and danger and disaster and rescue. After Small Dog left, Albert's parents went home. They needed to get some sleep, and so did Albert. Nurse's orders.

He slept much of that day and night and half of the next day. By late afternoon, he was feeling nearly like himself again. Albert was reading his track and field book when he heard a knock on the door. He rolled over to face the door. His cheek—punished by the rock wall—felt raw beneath its bandage, his scraped knee complained at the sudden movement. "Come in," he said.

The door opened, and Mr. Rockwood walked into the room, shoulders back, chin up, but smiling a real smile. Albert couldn't believe he was there.

"Albert, can you take one more visitor?"

"Sure." Albert sat up. That was about the closest to parade rest he could get. But Mr. Rockwood didn't look as if he expected any formalities. And he'd called him Albert.

"You've bounced back quickly. Your conditioning program paid off."

"I guess." Albert hadn't thought about it, but he supposed it had. "How did you know I was here?"

Mr. Rockwood smiled. "I've got my sources. One of them is very familiar with the origins of your baseball card, and also works for the newspaper."

Maggie. "How did she find out?"

"The story made news on the radio and television stations yesterday and today. They even interviewed your friend Lester. Tomorrow Maggie is going to do a story on you and Lester. She wants to come by and talk to you tonight, if you're up to it. She'll call your parents later."

"Did your sources tell you about my jump?"

"Of course. A chasm the width of the Grand Canyon, crossed in a single bold leap." He reached into a cloth bag and carefully pulled out a package. "In honor of which," he began ceremoniously, "and in recognition of your competence and good taste as a provider of reading enjoyment, and your willingness to help a sick woman despite her relationship with a curmudgeonly P.E. teacher, I present you with this small token of our appreciation and thanks." He gave the package to Albert. "Open it," he said.

"How did you know about the book?" Albert asked.

"'To Albert, the Most Precious Baby on Earth,'" Mr. Rockwood recited. "'Love, Aunt Bev.'" He smiled. "You forgot about the inscription."

Albert shook his head. What a genius he was. He carefully tore away the brown paper. Inside he found a small framed reproduction of the Bob Beamon poster—the one from the wall in Mr. Rockwood's office.

"This is for me?" Albert said.

"You earned it."

Albert stared at the poster, his mouth open. "I didn't do anything," he said.

"I found a package in my school mailbox this morning, Albert. It contained a remarkable amount of money—doubly remarkable, actually, in that it matched the value of a certain baseball card."

Albert felt his face growing hot.

"I first considered returning the money. But then I thought about the spirit in which the gift was given, and what this person had risked to give it. I decided that returning the money would be an insult. What do you think, Albert?"

"Does Mrs. Rockwood still need the money?"

"Mrs. Rockwood's medical expenses have put us in a financial hole deeper than the one you fell into. Unfortunately, the answer to your question is yes."

"Then the person who gave it to you would feel real bad if you didn't keep it."

"I thought so."

"How is she—Mrs. Rockwood, I mean?"

"She'll feel worse before she gets better, but at least now she has a chance. We think she has a good chance."

Albert stared at the poster before pulling it close to his chest. "Can you give one of these to Yuno? He out-jumped me yesterday. He was the real hero."

"I have one for him also."

"He'll love it."

"Would you mind telling me the whole story?" Mr. Rockwood asked. "I've heard the news version, but I have a feeling that I may have missed something. I'd like to hear about it from you." He pulled up a chair and straddled it backwards, looking at Albert, waiting for him to start.

Albert told him the story, from the day they discovered the card to the day he woke up in the hospital.

"Fascinating," Mr. Rockwood said. "You're a fortunate young man."

"I know."

Mr. Rockwood stood and glanced at the book on Albert's bed. "Track season begins in March. Think about it, Albert."

"I will."

"And Mrs. Rockwood and I will be thinking about you." He walked quickly from the room and closed the door quietly behind him.

Albert eased back down and laid his head on the pillow. He looked across the room at the wall clock: five-forty. He reached for the remote control, figuring that he should be able to find some news on TV. And if he could, maybe he'd see Yuno, maybe he'd hear him one more time.

Albert had heard Yuno's voice—felt it—knifing through the darkness of the mine, the blackness of his spirit. He'd listened to it as it pushed and prodded and coaxed him out of the depths, out of his would-be tomb, down the trail, down the highway. He could still hear it, as if it were last night. And he knew he wouldn't get tired of it anytime soon.

He lay on his back and scanned the channels. Through the thin blanket he could feel the weight of the poster on his chest. It felt good. He felt good. Maybe tonight he'd dream about jumping, about floating through the air with his arms spread wide, deciding where he wanted to land—if he wanted to land. He wanted to stay up there a long time.